Faster . . .

Frankie pulled Josh across the lawn, practically making him fall on his face. Josh caught up and grabbed her other arm. Together they swung each other around in a circle, bursting with joy. At first Frankie was aware of the curious stares from the people around her, then she saw only a blur as they went faster . . . faster. . . .

Before she knew it, they were on the ground, dissolving into dizzy, giddy laugher. But when Frankie looked over at Josh, she realized she was staring into the handsomest face she had ever seen.

COUPLES

COUPLES

FALLING FOR YOU

by M.E. Cooper

SCHOLASTIC INC.
New York Toronto London Auckland Sydney

ISBN 0-590-41265-5

12 11 10 9 8 7 6 5 4 3 2 1   8 9/8 0 1 2 3/9

Printed in the U.S.A.   01

First Scholastic printing, March 1988

Chapter
1

"WHO-O-O-A-A-A-H, OH, N-O-O-O-O!"
The walls shook from the loud music as Katie Crawford picked up a soggy onion ring from her plate. Slowly, she dipped it in the puddle of ketchup, then let it drop.

Her mind was a blank. There was just nothing left inside anymore, no feeling at all. She'd already screamed at everyone she knew — her mother, Greg, her best friend Molly.

They were the last people she wanted to be around now. She couldn't face all that pity in their eyes. Poor, pathetic Katie, they all seemed to be saying. She's looked so depressed since her skiing accident. What can we say to her? How should we act around her? It only made Katie feel worse, as if *she* now had to make *them* feel better.

All Katie wanted these days was to be lost in a crowd with people who didn't care who she was

1

and what had happened to her. Maybe that was why she'd ended up in the Hall of Fame. The place was kind of a dump, but at least here, she could hang out and be herself. Katie, her cast, and her crutches.

She looked around. On the walls were drawn black outlines of human figures in strange, frozen positions. They were poised either to attack or dance, Katie wasn't sure which. Someone's idea of art, she thought with a smirk. Above her, the ceiling was painted dark red. It made the room look gloomy, but kind of mysterious and inviting, too.

About twelve kids were dancing around the jukebox. They had funky hairstyles and most of them were wearing black, but other than that they just looked like normal kids.

At first, Katie had felt pretty weird about hanging out at the Hall of Fame. Not that she really knew anything about the place. None of her crowd would have ever dreamed of going there. And even if they *had* gone in, they wouldn't dare admit it. "The Hall of Shame," they'd always called it: a hangout for the punk rockers, the ripped leather jacket types, the losers. . . .

Which was exactly how Katie felt — like a total loser. She looked at the kids around her. No monogrammed sweaters, no conservative haircuts, no fake smiles. These kids looked like they wanted nothing to do with that boring world. And at this point, Katie felt just like them. Maybe being a "loser" wasn't so bad.

Katie stared blankly ahead of her, tired of her onion rings, tapping her hands to the beat of the blaring music. In her mind she was choreographing floor routines to the song. She imagined herself gliding across the mats to a burst of wild applause as the judges prepared to lift their score cards, each reading 10. That old, sweet familiar feeling swept through her: a feeling of being better, stronger, more graceful than anyone else.

Suddenly, though, reality came rushing back. Her mind was filled with the awful memories of the ski trip to Mount Jackson, and the burning, competitive streak in Roxanne Easton that had resulted in Katie's accident.

Even though Katie thought she couldn't possibly cry anymore, she felt the tears well up in her eyes. She shoved her plate against the wall of the booth. I can't keep thinking about it! she told herself. It's not going to make me feel any better!

But no matter how hard she tried, Katie couldn't stop the "if onlys" from racing through her mind. If only she hadn't insisted on everyone going down the advanced ski slope so she could show up Roxanne in front of Greg. . . . If only she'd gotten out the way when Eric fell in front of her. . . .

Katie shook her head and asked herself the same question for the millionth time: Of all the times this could have happened to her, why did she have to break her leg *now*? Her senior year; her last chance to compete — to go out in style. Without gymnastics, without anything to excel in, she was *nobody*. All her friends at Kennedy High — Molly, Eric, Karen, Holly, Brian — *they* could all still enjoy their senior year successes. But Katie couldn't, not anymore. She found it

3

harder and harder to look them in the face, harder to smile when the one thing that made her special was gone. At this point, the only thing she could do better than anyone else was walk on crutches.

She sank back into her seat and let out a deep, morose sigh. What was the use? No wonder her boyfriend, Greg Montgomery, seemed to be losing interest in her. Why would one of the cutest, smartest guys in the whole school stick around a girlfriend who couldn't do anything and was depressed all the time? A girlfriend who'd done nothing but yell at him for the last two months? There were more than enough lively, pretty girls around, especially now that Kennedy had merged with Stevenson High. Maybe Greg would be better off with someone like gorgeous transfer student Roxanne Easton.

Katie sighed again. She was back where she'd started, back to feeling nothing at all. Somehow that seemed to be the best thing. At least it didn't hurt.

Katie pushed back her sleeve to look at her watch. She still had lots of time to kill before her doctor's appointment. Fortunately she had had the sense to call the medical arts center across the parking lot to see if Dr. Merwin's other appointments were backed up, which they were. Katie's three forty-five appointment was postponed until a quarter of six. Well, at least she could say one good thing: this was the last day she'd ever have to drag herself around on crutches. The cast was *finally* coming off.

As she struggled to her feet to go get another soda, she caught sight of a blonde girl who was dancing in perfect rhythm with the pulsing beat. Katie recognized the girl. She had seen her at school, leaning against the walls between classes with her head down, sitting gloomily in the back of English class, going straight home after school. Nobody really knew her, as far as Katie could tell. She didn't seem to be the type to make a lot of friends. Rumor had it her family life was awful. Both her parents were alcoholics or something. She always looked blank, lifeless. But here, the girl looked so strong and . . . so *angry*.

The guy dancing with her had dark, spiky hair, and a cigarette in his hand. As he danced, he mumbled the words to the song. Katie watched his movements — they were quirky, rhythmic, expressive.

"Who-o-o-o-a!" Katie crumpled to the ground before she'd taken more than half a step. She clutched her leg in pain. The soda bottle she'd stepped on rolled quietly away.

"Are you all right?" a soft voice above her asked.

"It's okay . . . I have . . . another one!" Katie said, wincing and holding onto her cast as if it would make her sore leg feel better. She looked up to see the blonde girl and the dark-haired guy looking at her with concern.

"Here . . ." the boy said, reaching out.

"No, really," Katie answered, lifting herself up by grabbing the table. "It was my own fault. Thanks anyway."

"Your choice," he replied, smiling. He picked up the bottle from the floor. "You better be more careful where you put your diet soda!"

"What? That wasn't *my* — "

The guy laughed and began to move to the music again. "Just giving you a hard time." He gave her a friendly smile and turned back to the girl, who was also smiling.

Katie limped slowly toward the food counter. The pain was still shooting through her leg, but it was mixed with a crazy, pleasant feeling of relief. She'd finally run into someone who hadn't treated her like she was completely helpless. Katie wondered if all the kids who hung out there were like these two. Before she stepped up to place her order, she took a look back at the dance floor. The song on the jukebox was a hard-driving rock tune, and a bunch of kids were laughing and dancing to the music.

Katie smiled. They're a tough-looking bunch, she thought. But who would have thought they'd be so friendly and easygoing? No judgment, no competition, no jealousy. . . .

Slowly, a sad and confused look washed over Katie's face. Maybe I've been hanging out with the wrong crowd all along, she thought.

Chapter 2

For a brief moment, the student council room was absolutely still.

"Do you smell it?" Karen Davis said, with a blissful smile on her face.

"I sure do," answered Brian Pierson. He put an arm around his girlfriend. "What is it?"

Karen took another deep whiff of the scent that wafted through the open windows. "Cherry blossoms." She gave Brian a bear hug and buried her face in his neck. "Oooh, they just drive me crazy! Cherry blossoms are the first true sign of spring!"

"Okay you two, knock it off!" Greg Montgomery called out from the other side of the room. With a grin full of mock frustration, he held his hands out to the chairs scattered around the room. "I'll tell you what the first sign of spring is, it's trying to set up the first prom meeting of the year while everyone else is busy smelling cherry blossoms!"

"Oops, hands off or the set-up committee boss will fire us!" Brian said. He jumped away from Karen and took off around the room, straightening out chairs, sharpening pencils, and dusting off the table.

Greg threw his head back and laughed. "That's what I like to see — a dedicated worker! Come on, Brian! Faster! Faster!"

By this time, Karen was giggling so hard she had to sit down.

"*Nooo!*" Brian yelled to her. "You'll disturb the seating arrangement! Greg'll kill you!"

"Hey, come on!" Greg said. "I'm not that bad, am I?"

"No comment," Brian replied with a mischievous smile.

"Well, you know, it takes an incredible amount of work to set up a project like this," Greg retorted. He knew Brian was only trying to lighten things up, but somehow he felt a little defensive. There was something on his mind, something more important than the prom and the auction he was organizing to help pay for it. It was weighing him down, changing his usual confident, take-charge manner.

"And whose idea was this auction, hmm?" Brian said.

"Whose expensive idea was it to invite The Clangers to play at the prom?" Greg answered. He knew he'd made his point. The auction was the only way they could possibly raise enough money to keep prom ticket prices low and still cover the group's fee.

"He's right, Brian," Karen said. "Besides, it'll

be fun. You said so yourself. You're not having second thoughts about donating those old records, are you?"

"No, of course not," Brian said. He gave Greg a friendly punch on the shoulder. "I just like to get on Greg's case once in a while. There's got to be *somebody* in this school who doesn't always tell him he's perfect!"

Greg smiled, but inside he felt ripped apart. So perfect I can't even talk to my girlfriend, he said to himself. All he could think about these days was Katie. For these last few months, she'd been the most important thing in his life. Every day brought a new discovery about her, something new to love. It went beyond the way her eyes sparkled when she smiled, or the magical sound of her laughter. Success seemed to glow in the air around her. Her fierce competitiveness and confidence made him strive even harder to be the best. With her, everything had seemed possible . . . until the accident. All of a sudden he just couldn't do anything right. He'd tried to help her, but she wouldn't let him. But if he left her alone, she'd get mopey and jealous. That spunky, brave girl he'd been in love with was slowly disappearing. Every day he watched her shrink further into a shell, every day the sparkle dimmed from her eyes a little more. Maybe she thought she was covering up her pain, but he could see every moment of it in her face. No, not just see it — he could *feel* it. And the worst thing was that the whole situation was completely out of his control.

"Greg, are you okay?" Brian asked. "Really, I I was only kidding."

"Oh, I know, Brian." Greg snapped out of his gloom. This was definitely not the time to think about Katie. "I was just . . . uh, thinking about *my* auction promise. I don't know how I'm going to get my sailboat ready in time for the race."

Karen's eyes popped open. "You're auctioning off your precious *Sally Ride II*? All I'm putting up is a measly quarter-page ad in *The Red and the Gold*."

"No!" Greg laughed. "Not the boat. Just a ride in it during the Potomac River Fun Race!"

"Oh! For a moment there I thought you'd really gone overboard." Brian and Greg groaned at the bad pun, while Karen, who hadn't meant to say it, went right on talking. "Well," she said, "I still think a boat ride's a much more fun idea than mine."

"Don't sell yourself short," Brian said. "There are plenty of people in this school who would love to fill up that space in the newspaper with something — their own picture even!"

Karen batted her eyes in make-believe innocence. "Well now, *who* could you be talking about? It wouldn't be — "

"I won't mention any names," Brian said, raising his eyebrows and hunching over in an impersonation of Groucho Marx, "but her initials are Roxanne Easton!"

"Come on, she's really not that bad," Greg argued. "In fact, she's the only one of the Stevenson kids who told me she'd try to come to the meeting."

"The key word there is *try*," Brian said. "No

10

real commitment. I think the Stevenson gang still thinks our crowd is a bunch of snobs."

Greg shrugged his shoulders and shook his head. Ever since the two schools merged this winter, everyone had made an effort to make the kids from Stevenson High feel welcome. Greg couldn't imagine how his friends could have tried harder to be friendly. Sure, they were the top group in the school, the leaders in all the activities, but they'd been going out of their way to include the Stevenson students. Something just didn't seem right. "I thought that would all be over by now," he said. "Especially after Karen's great interview with Lily in the newspaper."

"The interview was a step in the right direction," Karen said, "but that's about it. The Stevenson kids were pretty happy to read about one of their own, though. A lot of them even complimented me on the article."

"They *should*," Brian said. "Let's face it, Lily Rorshak's life story is mind-boggling! Even *I* almost cried. I mean, the way she cleaned up her life after living on the streets and all the trouble she was in. . . . And you made her sound so brave, so determined."

"Thanks," Karen said with a smile. "But the fact is, Brian, one article isn't going to end all the tension between the two schools. They still sense that our group runs everything at Kennedy, and they don't feel accepted here. Jonathan's party was a good start, but we're just going to have to work harder to include them."

The three of them were talking so intently, no

one seemed to notice the door open behind them.

"Work harder?" a voice said. "That work-aholic Greg must be rubbing off on you. This place looks terrific!"

They turned to see Colin Edwards walking into the room, carrying a leather and canvas shoulder bag. He had an air of hurried importance, like someone who realized he was always in demand. On his face was a slightly sheepish grin.

Brian looked at his watch. "What is this, executive privilege? The student council president doesn't show up until after all the work is done!"

"Sorry, Brian," Colin apologized with a laugh. "My tutoring session ran late. The room looks great. Did you guys have any problems?"

"Aside from getting Greg to loosen up, no," Brian answered.

"You're kidding. That doesn't sound like the Greg Montgomery *I* know." Colin turned toward Greg.

Greg could just hear the "What's the matter with you?" about to come out of his friend's mouth, so he quickly changed the subject. "So, have you spoken to any of the Stevenson bunch lately? Do you think they'll come? Why isn't anyone here yet?"

"Is *that* what you're worried about?" Colin said. "Look, I'm sure we'll get a few of those Stevenson kids in for the meeting. That's all we need. Word of mouth will take care of the rest. Believe me, soon everyone in the school will be talking about this thing. And I guarantee that by the time of the auction, they'll all be involved."

At that moment, they began to hear footsteps

12

and voices in the hall. Colin looked at his watch and walked to the head of the long conference table. "Cheer up, Greg," he continued. "Here they come."

Colin reached into his shoulder bag, pulled out several pages of stapled-together notes, and put them down on the table. Karen and Brian took seats on either side of him. About ten empty chairs stood ready around the table.

Greg greeted people as they walked in. He was surprised at how many people had come, especially on a day like today. A warm spring breeze was wafting through the hallway, beckoning everyone outside. But it didn't seem to matter. All the familiar faces were there, juniors and seniors alike: Molly Ramirez, Colin's brother Rich, Holly Daniels. . . . Before long, all the seats around the table were taken.

Karen walked up to Greg and whispered, "No one from Stevenson yet. Colin says he'll wait about five more minutes."

During those five minutes, the room filled to bursting with laughing, giddy students — spring fever was unmistakably in the air. Brian and Karen unfolded a half dozen extra chairs, and by the time Colin began to speak, there were even a couple of students standing in the doorway.

"What a great start!" Colin said, to open the meeting. "Judging from today's response, it looks like we'll have no trouble drumming up enthusiasm for this auction. . . ."

Looking around the room, Greg realized this was only partly true. He scanned the faces. They were all friendly, all familiar — but all were dyed-in-the-wool Kennedy High students, too. It was worse than he'd thought it would be. Of course, the Stevenson kids couldn't be expected to show up in full force, but he didn't think *none* of them would come.

"We each have something in our lives that would be valuable to others," Colin was saying to the gathering. "Something that people would bid on at our auction. Brian Pierson, as we all know, runs WKND. He has offered to let us auction off an old collection of jazz records. Diana Einerson has told me she'll offer a horseback-riding lesson. . . ."

Greg couldn't concentrate on a word Colin said. He sat there silently, trying desperately to look like his old, carefree self. But a huge feeling of disappointment was beginning to smother him. And it didn't have anything to do with the lack of Stevenson students.

There was someone else who wasn't at the meeting, someone far more important than anyone from Stevenson. Katie Crawford was nowhere to be seen.

At first he was worried. Maybe she fell down. Maybe her leg was hurting too much to come. But no, that couldn't be it. Someone would have told him. . . .

Suddenly it dawned on him — she was supposed to get her cast off today at three forty-five! A feeling of relief rushed over him. He was sure that would pick up her spirits. And she'd probably be coming to the meeting afterward.

Greg checked his watch. It was only four forty-five. She'd just be done by now. For the

14

first time, he could smell the cherry blossoms and hear Colin's boring speech. *I shouldn't worry so much about her,* he thought. *Just give her all the love and support I can.* A smile crept across his face as he looked down at his open loose-leaf notebook. There was really nothing Colin was saying that he needed to write down, so he took out a crisp, blank page and drew a quick cartoon of Kennedy High at the bottom. On the roof he put two handles, making JFK look like a gymnastics horse. Off to one corner, he sketched a shabby, discarded pair of crutches. Then, carefully, he drew Katie. Like a gymnastics superwoman, she loomed above the school, swinging over the high school horse in perfect form. Her once-broken leg was now mended and strong, and her face showed the grit and determination he had seen so often in the past. Around the school, tiny students looked up in admiration and amazement.

Greg chuckled at the finished drawing and looked out into the empty hallway. This would really give Katie's spirits a boost.

By the time Colin opened the floor for discussion, it was five-fifteen. Just about everyone had comments and suggestions. Brian had kept notes at the meeting, and Karen helped him take down all the items that everyone wanted to auction off.

"This is incredible, Greg. You're a genius!" Karen said as she scribbled furiously. "Everyone wants to donate something!"

"Yeah, but nobody's volunteering to help out with publicity," Brian added.

"I'll handle it," said Greg. Looking around at

the enthusiastic crowd, a feeling of triumph came over him. This was his idea, and it was working. "Hey, everyone," he called out, "I'll volunteer to coordinate the publicity, but I need a team of co-coordinators to write ads for the radio and blitz the school with posters. It'll only take a few minutes each day, and your names will be printed on the programs. . . ."

Almost instantly he had about five volunteers. Within a half hour, all the positions of responsibility for the auction were filled, and Colin adjourned the meeting with a broad grin on his face.

A few students stuck around to talk, but most began to straggle out to go home. Greg took a look at his watch. A sudden empty sensation made him slump into a chair.

It was already six o'clock. Maybe Katie had forgotten, but he didn't think so. Greg thought about Katie's dark moods, about the way she'd been putting him off this past month. Maybe she just didn't feel like being around him anymore.

Chapter
3

Roxanne Easton was furious. She was trying not to let it show, but it was pretty obvious. Anyone could tell from the way she was standing. Her back was as straight as the flagpole, and she let the wind blow strands of her silken auburn hair across her eyes as her glance darted up and down the street. In fact, only one other part of her body moved — her foot, which she was tapping slightly in irritation.

"It must be about five o'clock, huh?" she said coolly.

Frankie Baker nodded. Seeing her best friend like this always made her nervous. She could recognize the signs of Roxanne losing her temper a mile away. For a while, Rox would say very little, pretend to be above it all. Then, without warning, she'd blow up, just explode. Not that Frankie blamed her this time; after all, Mrs.

Easton *had* completely ruined Roxanne's after-school plans.

Frankie folded and unfolded her arms. She knew she should say *something*; the silence was killing her. But what? Her thoughts raced around in her head. Out of the corner of her eye she caught Roxanne looking at her.

Frankie felt herself take an unexpected gulp of air. "Uh, what time did your mom say she'd pick you up?"

"Four-fifteen. I already told you that," Roxanne said.

"Oh. Oh, that's right. Well, maybe they got her message wrong at the front desk. Maybe she meant five-fifteen."

Roxanne rolled her eyes and let out a weary sigh. "You know, Frankie, for all that incredible brainpower of yours, sometimes you can be so naive. You know she pulls this stunt all the time. How many times did I end up waiting for her at Stevenson? Remember? And it seems like it's always happening here, too."

Frankie shrugged and nodded. She really wasn't *stupid* or anything; she only got like this around Roxanne. And yet she felt sorry for her friend. Parents weren't supposed to be irresponsible like this.

"I can just hear the excuse, too," Roxanne continued. She tipped her nose in the air and put on a husky, bored-sounding voice. " 'Awfully sorry, sweetheart, but Mrs. Pignostril was showing me this absolutely *exquisite* collection of Ming vases, and, well, it was *dreadfully* hard to break away. Especially when she got her fat, flabby arm stuck inside one. You see, she thought she had dropped some of those *marvelous* chocolate truffles inside.' "

Frankie couldn't keep herself from giggling.

"Then she'll tell me she didn't know the phone number at school. But of *course* she knew it when she needed it to call and tell me in the middle of the day that I had to meet her after school. Does she tell me in person? No. Does she consider that maybe I had plans? No!"

"I know, it's really unfair of her. Maybe you should — " Frankie squinted. In the distance, a shiny foreign car turned a corner toward them. "Here she comes now, I think. Look, I have an idea — "

Roxanne rushed out to the curb and peered up the street, a look of annoyance on her face. But the look turned to anger as she spotted the sleek black car.

"That's a Porsche. My mother drives a BMW!" Roxanne said, practically spitting out her words. She slammed her books down on the sidewalk.

Here she goes. There's no stopping her now, Frankie thought. "Roxanne, why don't you just sit down with your mother this weekend and tell her how you feel?"

"When? She's shipping Torrey and me off to Dad's for the weekend! And if I bring up anything in the car, Torrey will just turn up that stupid radio station and drown me out!"

"Well, what about telling your father about it?"

Roxanne threw up her hands. "Great suggestion. I'll get to see the old Rushmore effect again."

19

Frankie hated when Roxanne said mysterious things like that, just assuming she'd understand what they meant. "Uh . . . what are you talking about?" she asked.

"That's the way he gets when I have a problem. Like those old stone faces at Mount Rushmore. He'll just get all worried and brood about it for a few days. Then, a week later, there'll be a half-dozen roses waiting for me at Mom's house, or a box of chocolates that Torrey's already eaten, or — if I'm lucky — some ugly skirt or shirt that doesn't fit. Mom'll storm up to her room and scream at his answering machine about how he's trying to 'buy my love,' and then the whole subject will be forgotten until the next time it happens!"

As Roxanne paced back and forth, Frankie paced with her. "Well, at least he tries."

"Yeah? Well, I hate it," Roxanne muttered. "I feel like something from a mail-order catalog, going back and forth from one house to the other." She pulled back her sleeve to look at her watch. Suddenly a cry of frustration escaped her mouth. "Aaaagh! Five-fifteen! This is so cruel! I could have even gone to that stupid prom meeting!"

"Is *that* where you wanted to go?" Frankie said. "I thought — "

"I know, it's probably full of all those boring goody-goody gung-ho types planning that auction or whatever. But I was *dying* to see that incredible hunk." She sighed. "I had it all worked out."

Frankie wasn't sure which guy Roxanne had

her eye on now. "What hunk? You don't mean. . . ."

"Oh, please!" Roxanne laughed. "Don't worry, Frankie, your old jock heartthrob is safe for the moment!"

Frankie felt her face turning red with embarrassment. How did Rox know she meant Zachary McGraw? "You told me you thought Zack was cute."

"Well, yeah, he's *cute*, but . . . well. . . ." Roxanne shrugged her shoulders. "Not *really* hunky, like Greg Montgomery! I mean, haven't you noticed how everybody just seems to flock around him? Anyway, he's one of the organizers of that meeting."

"Wait a minute, I don't get it. You've been telling all the Stevenson kids to stay away from this meeting. If you like Greg so much, don't you think he'd be more impressed if you got everyone to go?"

"But that's just it, I *will* get them to go. Right now that whole crowd from Kennedy is paranoid that the Stevenson kids hate them. So when no one at all from Stevenson shows up at the meeting, their worst fears will have come true, right?" She smiled, obviously pleased. "They'll be *dying* for someone to act as a peacemaker between the schools."

"Isn't that unfair? I mean, you *kept* everyone away in the first place!"

Roxanne shook her head. "Nobody forced them. Look, they didn't feel like going anyway, and I just told them I agreed with them."

"I — I don't know, Rox. Maybe you're right, but still. . . ."

"Oh, Frankie, you're so straitlaced! I think it's a great plan." She gave her friend a meaningful smile. "And if Greg Montgomery happens to be impressed by it . . . well, then everybody wins! Right?"

Everybody except Katie, Frankie thought. She hated it when Roxanne was devious like this. Every time it happened, she vowed to stand up to her. But each time she just couldn't bring herself to do it — logic always won out. Even though her conscience often nagged at her to tell Roxanne off, her mind warned her it just didn't make sense. What would she gain? Maybe a little peace of mind. But she would lose her best friend. No, her *only* friend, really.

Roxanne gave Frankie a knowing glance. "I know you're thinking about Greg's girlfriend, right?"

Frankie turned red again. She didn't think she was *that* transparent.

"I've been watching them," Roxanne went on. "It's over, I know it. She doesn't even give him the time of day anymore."

"But he's *so* hung up on her!"

"You mean *was*. No guy can put up with the kind of abuse she's been dishing out for very long. I mean, let's face it, she stood him up at the debate tournament *and* the Maple Sugarin' Festival! And . . . there's been this little flicker of interest in his eyes lately when we've talked." She winked slyly. "I can tell these things."

Frankie sighed to herself. She wished she could

say the same thing about guys. Sure, she knew she had strong points, but they had nothing to do with love. Computers were so much easier to figure out, and they didn't ever make you nervous or look right through you as if you didn't exist. Frankie was sure she wouldn't even be able to tell if anyone actually was interested in her, not that there had ever *been* anyone. Roxanne was so different — so beautiful, so sexy. It seemed all she had to do was throw back her hair and give the tiniest smile, and guys would fall all over themselves to please her. If Frankie ever tried anything like that, they'd just think she was being weird.

"Besides," Roxanne went on about Greg, "I need a date for the prom, and why not go for the best? Don't you think he'll ask me, if I can get everyone from Stevenson involved in the prom plans?"

"I don't know, Rox. I'm still not sure he's over Katie."

In a flash, Roxanne spun around. Her green eyes pierced into Frankie's. "And what would *you* know about it?" She planted her hands on her hips. "Who's *your* prom date, might I ask? Or are you still trying to decide which offer to take?"

Frankie had known this was coming. Whenever Roxanne got angry, it always seemed to wind around to the same thing.

"Let's see," Roxanne continued meanly, putting her hand on her chin. "Could it possibly be . . ."

Frankie felt like melting into the ground. Why did she have to do this?

". . . Zachary McGraw?" Roxanne pretended to swoon. "That cute, muscular football hero who always seems to need math tutoring? Hmm? What exactly do you two do in those *tutoring* sessions?"

Frankie's face was flaming. She turned around and looked down at the sidewalk.

Roxanne giggled. "Oh, come on, you know I'm just kidding. Relax."

Yeah, right, Frankie thought. She wished she had the courage to turn around and stomp away.

Just then a high-pitched honk sounded from across the street.

"Hi, sweetheart! I'm here!" a voice rang out.

Mrs. Easton. At least I'm saved from any more humiliation, Frankie thought. She waved to Mrs. Easton. Roxanne's mother was even more glamorous than her daughter. Her white-blonde hair glowed in the early evening sun as she quickly waved back and said to Rox, "Hurry, dear. I'm already very late!"

Roxanne slowly picked up her books from the sidewalk, one by one. Frankie knew she was taking her time on purpose.

"Listen, Frankie," Roxanne whispered. "Would you do me a favor?" Without waiting for an answer, she went on: "Just hang out by the student council room until the meeting is over — it shouldn't be too long. When Greg comes out, tell him what happened with my mother. Tell him I was really upset that I couldn't be at the meeting, and I'll do *anything* to make the fund raiser a success."

This was too much, Frankie thought. Roxanne knew how shy she was around guys, let alone big shots like Greg Montgomery. And besides, what did Rox think she was anyway, her messenger?

24

Frankie wanted to flat-out refuse, but instead she hedged. "I don't know, Roxanne. I've got this big math test to study for . . . and anyway, *you* can tell Greg tomorrow, can't you?"

Mrs. Easton blew the BMW's horn again. "Come on, dear, you can talk to Frankie over the phone at Dad's."

"I'll be right there," Roxanne shouted. She shot a betrayed look at Frankie. "I'm under all this pressure and you won't do this for me? After all I've done for you? I'll remember this, Frankie." She picked up her last book and began to cross the street. "I don't know why you just want to throw this friendship away. I mean, how many other friends do you have, Frankie? You'll have no social life at all if you drop me like this. . . ."

Frankie couldn't bear it when Roxanne said things like that. Much as she didn't like to admit it, Roxanne was right. "Oh, okay," Frankie said softly, following her friend.

"What?" Roxanne called over her shoulder.

"I said I'll do it."

Roxanne opened the car door and slid into the plush front seat. She smiled up at Frankie. "Thanks. I knew I could count on you."

With that, the BMW sped off.

Feeling angry and disappointed in herself, Frankie slumped back toward the school entrance.

Chapter 4

"*P*ignatale, dear. Not Pignostril. Be nice."

Roxanne folded her arms and stared straight ahead through the window. How she wished she could just jump out of the car and run away forever — away from her mother, her crazy brother, the town of Rose Hill, Mrs. Pignatale, *everything.* . . .

"I don't care *what* her name is," she answered. "I was waiting for a whole hour . . . and there was something I wanted to do after school!"

"Well, Rox, people can't always do exactly what they want. Just do it first thing next week."

Roxanne squirmed in her seat and leaned out the side window. "Oh, you'll never understand."

"I said the same thing to my mother when I was your age." Mrs. Easton took a long drag on her cigarette. "Look, do you think I'm happy that I'm running late? Do you think I *want* to drive you and your brother all the way to Sandy

Hill again? I'm only doing this because I have to catch an earlier flight to New York."

"New York? Are you seeing that creepy real estate guy again?"

"Henry Simone is not creepy, Roxanne. And, I might add, if you were a little nicer to him, maybe I'd invite him here more often instead of going away all the time!"

Roxanne didn't answer. Which was better — putting up with her mother's carelessness or dealing with that pompous, cigar-smoking idiot all weekend? "I just don't know what you see in him, Mom."

"Henry is a perfectly wonderful man."

"Henry is a perfectly *rich* man," Roxanne said sarcastically.

Mrs. Easton chuckled. "Well, sweetheart, if a man happens to make a good living, that's certainly no reason to turn my nose up at him, is it?" She gave her daughter a sidelong glance from under her sunglasses. "After all, why not go for the best?"

Roxanne felt like screaming. Her mother never thought of anyone but herself. She hadn't even asked her about her day at school. As usual, she couldn't talk about anything but her own social life. Roxanne had half a mind to tell her something completely outrageous, like, "The school doctor told me I have a brain tumor." Her mother would probably puff on her cigarette, think for a minute, and say, "That reminds me . . . do you remember that tall brain surgeon I was seeing? He got married last week, to his receptionist. Can you believe it?"

Roxanne looked at her mother as she drove calmly through the streets of Rose Hill. With her hair waving gently in the wind, she looked so gorgeous, so young — people sometimes thought they were sisters. Roxanne sighed. Too bad she wasn't really her sister. Then maybe she'd pay more attention to her. Maybe she'd treat her like an adult instead of a worthless, pesty little girl. What an insult that she wanted to spend more time with that Simone jerk than with her own daughter. She said she was "going for the best." Well, Roxanne decided, she would show her mother what the best was all about!

"Guess what, Mom? I think I'm going to the prom with Greg Montgomery!"

"Greg who, darling?"

"Montgomery! You know, the one you said looked like Rob Lowe?"

"Well, just make sure he has a car. I'm not going to want you driving around in the BMW until the crack of dawn."

Before Roxanne could protest, Mrs. Easton said, "Okay, here we are. Go in and get your brother — and do it quickly, before one of those hoodlums slashes my tires."

Roxanne's jaw dropped when she saw where they'd stopped. An outdoor shopping plaza stretched out before them. The old tan brick mall had gotten pretty run down since the big indoor mall opened. At the far end of it, a group of rough-looking teenagers dressed in black were sitting on the hood of an old Chevy. They were giving her mother's car the eye. Behind them, next to a shop that had been boarded up for years, was a dark, open doorway. The words HALL OF FAME were written above the doorway in big letters that looked like graffiti. Someone had crossed out the letter F in FAME and written SH above it so the name looked like HALL OF SHAME. Ear-splitting music blasted out from inside.

"You're kidding," Roxanne cried in disbelief. "I'm not going in there! What if someone sees me?"

Mrs. Easton gave her a stern look. "Well, then who will? Do you expect *me* to go in there? What would Torrey do if he saw his mother walk into the Hall of Fame? We'd never see him again!"

"But Mom, that place is disgusting! Look at those creeps outside! And they're probably the kids who are too scared to go in."

"Roxanne, what a thing to say! Are you forgetting that your brother is in there?"

"*You're* the one who lets him hang out in that sleazy place! No wonder he's such a basket case."

Roxanne could see that her mother was getting angry. In a strange way, it made her feel *good*. At least she'd gotten some sort of emotional reaction from her.

"Well, I don't see *you* including Torrey with your friends. You're always talking about the nice boys you know, the student council this, the editor of that . . . I would think you'd introduce them to your brother. Your poor brother, who's had such a hard time mixing with the right kind of people. But no, you turn your back on him. Is it any wonder he's always in trouble?"

I can't believe she's blaming me, Roxanne thought. "Mom, I don't know what you're talking about! First of all, Torrey's only a sophomore. He's too immature to hang out with my friends. Besides, I'm in a new school now, remember? I want to make a good impression. Everyone would run away if they saw me walking down the hall with Conan the Barbarian."

"Look, Roxanne, I don't have the time — "

"And besides, he's so *negative* all the time. You should see what happens to the few nice people he manages to meet. They turn into screw-ups, too!"

"Enough!" her mother screamed. "I will *not* take the blame for your brother's behavior. Now I don't want to hear another word. Go!"

Roxanne got out of the car and slammed the door. With a look of utter disgust on her face, she walked toward the Hall of Fame.

The eyes of all the nearby boys followed her. "Hey, nice wheels you got!" one of them yelled. "They yours or your big sister's?"

The ultimate insult. Roxanne could just imagine her mother sitting in the car, gloating to herself about the compliment. They're not such bad kids after all, she'd be thinking.

"She's my grandmother!" Rox called back as she walked into the club.

The music inside the Hall of Fame was so loud it made Roxanne's teeth vibrate. She couldn't imagine how anyone could carry on a conversation. It doesn't matter to them, anyway, she thought. They probably don't have anything to talk about.

A look of distaste on her face, she glanced around the dark room. It was hard to see anything because of the cigarette smoke and all the bodies dancing around. "Excuse me!" she called out, pushing her way through the crowd. But no one heard her; they all seemed to be trying to yell louder than the music.

Suddenly Roxanne did a double take. That *couldn't* be who she thought it was. Not here. She sneaked up a little closer.

Amazing. From the back, it sure looked like her. Same red hair, at least. The girl leaned back, and Roxanne stepped back against the wall. She didn't want some strange kid to think she was snooping. For all she knew, it might even be a guy — you could never tell in this place.

That's when she saw the crutches — the well-worn, *short* crutches. They could only have belonged to someone who was not much taller than five feet. There was no doubt in Rox's mind now.

Katie Crawford, she said to herself. A devilish grin crossed her face. Could this be her secret, underground social life? What an interesting development. She crossed over to the pinball machine near the far wall, where she had a clearer view.

It was Katie, all right. She was sitting glumly by herself, fiddling with a straw, looking around. What is she doing in here? Roxanne wondered. She moved a little closer. Of everyone there, Katie seemed to be the only one who wasn't moving around and talking. She was the only one who was alone, too. Roxanne could tell in a second that she was depressed. Still, after all this time. Her face looked drawn and gloomy, so different from the way she'd always looked before that accident at Mount Jackson. For a second,

31

Roxanne felt a twinge of pity. Katie had really been through a lot these past few months. Rox knew her life had revolved around gymnastics, and it must have felt terrible to have to quit the team.

But Rox still couldn't figure out why on earth she was at the Hall of Fame. She watched as Katie checked her watch, swallowed the rest of her soda, and reached for her crutches.

Quickly, Roxanne turned toward the pinball machine and pretended to play, as Katie slowly made her way to the door.

"Oh, no!" a rough, masculine voice shouted from somewhere nearby. "There goes the neighborhood! What are *you* doing here?"

Roxanne gasped and swung around. Staring at her was a broad-shouldered guy with very short, dark, spiky hair. He was handsome in a tough-guy sort of way, but the look in his eyes was mostly one of surprise.

"Guess where we're going this weekend, Torrey?" Roxanne said, rolling her eyes.

Torrey let out a loud groan. "No *way! Now* she tells us? What does she think we are?"

"That's just what I said, but you know how much good arguing is going to do. . . ."

"Is she just *sitting* out there?"

He was answered by the sound of a horn honking outside.

The two of them looked at each other. Neither one could keep back a grin. "She's in a hurry tonight, huh?" Torrey said.

Roxanne nodded.

"Good. Let's make her wait." He sat at a booth

and gestured for Roxanne to take a seat opposite him. Roxanne slid onto the bench and leaned eagerly across the table.

"Torrey, I *have* to ask you something. And promise me you'll give me a serious answer."

"You know what Mom says, 'Only fools and lawyers ask for promises.' "

"Okay, forget it. Just tell me if you remember seeing a red-haired girl with a broken leg in here before, real small, athletic-looking. . . ."

"I'm dating her."

Roxanne's eyes bugged out. "You are?"

"Yeah, we're eloping next year. We're going to tour the country in our own rock group. I'll do lead vocals, and she'll play the drums with her crutches."

Roxanne looked off into the distance with angry, pursed lips. She hated it when he did this. "Come on, I'm serious. She just left."

"What's it to you?" he said. Then he sat back and thought for a minute. "Yeah, I've seen her here before. She's pretty cute. I think she's only been here a couple of times. This doesn't seem like her kind of place." He narrowed his eyes. "Oh, I get it — she's one of your wimpy robot friends like Frankie, right?"

"Knock it off, Torrey."

"And you want to track her down so she can do your homework tonight," he continued. "What'd she do, get her leg stuck in a disk drive?" He laughed at his joke.

Roxanne knew if she wanted to, she could verbally tear her brother apart, but instead she sat back and thought for a minute.

A feeling of excitement began to grow inside her. Greg would absolutely freak if he knew Katie was here, she thought. There must be a way to make sure he found out. But that would be tough. What would Greg think of *her* if he knew she had been to the Hall of Shame?

Suddenly she was hit by a brilliant idea. In Katie's present state of mind, she was probably a sitting duck for someone cynical and negative . . . someone like Torrey. And he *was* pretty good-looking. If Roxanne could only hook the two of them up, there would be no way Greg would ever want to see Katie again.

"She's not really a friend," Roxanne said, turning back to her brother. She shrugged her shoulders. "Anyway, she got what she deserved."

"You mean her broken leg? Why did she deserve it?" he said, yawning.

Rox knew she had to do this carefully. If he so much as *suspected* what she was up to, he'd be sure to do the opposite of what she wanted.

"Well, she's been really rotten to her boyfriend since she broke her leg. She acts like it's the end of the world, and then yells at him when he tries to help. I hear he dumped her today."

"Oh, you really like that kind of stuff, don't you?" Torrey said, giving her a disgusted look. "That meaningless upperclassman gossip. Her boyfriend's probably a creep."

"Well, she's no great shakes herself," Roxanne said. "I mean, she comes *here*, doesn't she?"

"And what's that supposed to mean?" he snapped back. "I've got news for you — she's a lot better-looking than you!" He stood up from

34

the table. "In fact, I hope she comes here again. I'd like to get to know her!" With a toss of his head, he beckoned Roxanne to follow him. "Let's go, before Mom has a heart attack."

Roxanne tingled inside. She watched as Torrey shuffled out the door with a smug grin on his face. It's working, she said to herself. Her feet barely touched the ground as she skipped out the door. Who'd have thought getting Greg Montgomery would be so easy?

Chapter 5

```
DATA  ERROR  0238
INSERT  CORRECT  DISK  IN  DRIVE  B
```

Not again! What could she have done wrong? Frankie wondered. She ejected the disk from her computer and looked at it. This is really stupid, she thought. It's upside down.

Frankie wasn't used to having so much trouble with the computer. It scared her. *Guys* were what she was clumsy with, not computers.

She looked at her watch. Six o'clock. She felt beads of sweat forming inside her collar. How could she stall any longer? Greg's meeting *must* be over by now. Slowly she reached for the surge suppressor and clicked off the computer. She walked over to a shelf, pulled off a dust cover, and carefully draped it over the machine.

For a long moment she considered going home. After all, what did she really owe Roxanne, anyway? She offered Rox her friendship, and all she got in return were threats. It was as though she were under a spell or something. She turned and started to walk away, wondering if she'd ever dare break away from Roxanne, if she'd ever have a best friend who didn't use her all the time. Any normal person would say I was right if I just walked home right now, Frankie told herself. She drew herself up to her full five feet five. A feeling of strength came over her. Right then and there, she resolved never to take orders from Roxanne again. She'd teach her a lesson! Let her do her own dirty work for once!

But as soon as Frankie reached her decision, she began to feel afraid. She was afraid of not having even one friend anymore, of never being able to meet any of the Kennedy kids without Roxanne to introduce her around. Then another image flipped into her mind. It was a picture of Roxanne, on the verge of crying, looking up the street for the car that was an hour late. Who was Frankie kidding? Roxanne needed her. Even though she wasn't perfect, she was still Frankie's best friend.

Frankie lingered by the computer for a moment, as if it might give her courage a boost. Okay, Baker, she said to herself. Time to face the music. You can't go back on your agreement now. With an extra-brave look on her face, she walked toward the door. She shut off the light, took one last look into the Kennedy High Computer Center, and started down the hall.

It was the third time that day that Frankie had rounded the corner into the school's west wing. And it was the third time she'd heard voices coming from the student council room. But this time there weren't quite so many voices, and the noise wasn't as loud. She also heard laughter and the shuffling of papers, but Frankie could tell the meeting was over.

"This is going to be much bigger than we expected," one voice said.

"Do you think we'll have to use the large auditorium?" the other voice replied.

Frankie walked up the hall and stood in the doorway. Only Holly and Diana were still there, and they were so busy gabbing they didn't notice her. She cleared her throat. Still no reaction. Finally she gave a few little raps on the door.

Both girls turned around. "Hi, Frankie!" Holly called out.

Frankie smiled back shyly.

"Come on in. We were just talking about the the auction," Diana said, pulling up a chair. "It's too bad you didn't come earlier. You missed the *best* meeting!"

"But it really doesn't matter," Holly added quickly. "If you want to help with the auction plans or donate something, there's still time to sign up."

Frankie took a tentative step into the room. "Uh . . . thanks, maybe I will. Is, um, is Greg around?"

"No, he's still working, of course," Holly answered with a laugh. "He and Brian went over to WKND to write some promo ads for the auction. You know where that is?"

"Yes. Thanks," Frankie said and started to turn away. " 'Bye."

"See you," Diana said. "Come to our next meeting if you want. The date will be posted on the bulletin board."

"Okay," Frankie said and waved to them.

They're so friendly, she thought as she walked down the hall. How could anyone believe that people like Diana and Holly were snobs? It seemed so unfair that Roxanne was trying to alienate the Stevenson crowd from them. And for such a dumb reason — she was just going to turn right around and try to get the two crowds together. What if it didn't work? she suddenly thought. What if Roxanne had done such a good job that their school would *always* hate the Kennedy kids? There might not be enough time to patch things up. After all, summer vacation started in less than two months.

Frankie was so lost in thought that she walked right by the WKND office. It wasn't until she heard a wild blast of singing that she snapped back to reality.

It was "Big Time," by Peter Gabriel, and it was very loud. And way out of tune. She approached the office and stood in the doorway. A curly-haired guy with glasses was singing and dancing around the room. In rhythm to the music, he took records and tapes off a table and put them on shelves. Frankie stood in the doorway, feeling stuck. She couldn't leave, but if she knocked, she might embarrass him.

Finally, on the last note of the song, he spun around and dropped to one knee — right in front of Frankie.

"Whoa! I didn't know I had an audience," he said, scrambling to his feet.

"Sorry!" Frankie blurted. "I didn't mean to — "

"Sorry?" he said, grinning. "Are you kidding? This is a great honor. Do you know how hard it is to get people to listen to me? Usually I clear a room!"

For the first time all day, Frankie felt herself relax. Just looking at this guy made her want to smile. He seemed so kind and open. Not terrific-looking like Zack, but definitely cute. There was something special about his eyes. They had a warmth and tenderness she hadn't seen in too many guys — at least not when they looked at *her*.

"I thought you were pretty good. Maybe you ought to take lessons," she offered with a shrug.

The guy clasped his hands to his chest, threw back his head, and exclaimed, "Yes! His perfor-mance draws a huge response from the crowd! Ladies and gentlemen, Josh Ferguson, from the humble town of Raspberry Patch, U.S.A., has drawn a standing ovation from a sell-out crowd at the Kennedy Center!"

Frankie couldn't help giggling. "Well, I wouldn't go *that* far."

"All right, all right," Josh said, throwing up his hands, "A small but intimate group at Carnegie Hall. Come on in." He led Frankie into the office.

"Is Greg Montgomery around?" she asked, remembering why she was there.

"You just missed him. He was here with Brian, writing this corny ad for the junior/senior prom. I think they both went home."

Frankie felt relieved. At least I can tell Roxanne I tried, she thought. Gazing around the office, she saw shelves crammed full of record albums and cassettes. Two worn-out armchairs faced each other, and across from them was a long desk that had some very complex-looking sound equipment. In front of the desk, a wide, thick window looked into a tiny broadcast booth with a table and a microphone.

"This is a neat place," she said. "Do you work here?"

"Do I work here?" Josh repeated, his eyes widening in mock disbelief. "You are privileged to be in the company of the future director of world-famous WKND radio station and creator of the acclaimed *Cloaks and Jokes* program."

"I *figured* you did that show!" Frankie said. "Those stories you tell are really funny. Do you write them all yourself?" She was surprised that she could talk to Josh so easily. Usually when she was around guys, Frankie got all nervous and froze up.

"Sure do. You like them?" Josh said, looking sincerely flattered.

"Yes. Especially the ones about that small town — "

"Raspberry Patch, U.S.A.!" he said with glee.

41

"I'm glad you listen to those. They're based on the place I used to live."

"Really? I didn't know places like that existed anymore — places with soda fountains, community centers, barn dances. . . ."

Josh laughed. "There's a whole other world outside of suburbia. People where I come from think any building over six stories is a skyscraper."

"Well, you sure know how to get across the flavor of the place."

The grin on Josh's face was so broad, Frankie thought his cheeks would break. "Thanks!" he said. "You have no idea how much it means to hear that. I haven't admitted this to many people, but my dream is to do this kind of thing for a living, on national radio." His eyes shone warmly at her. Suddenly, he said, "You know, you haven't even told me your name."

Frankie felt herself blushing, and she couldn't quite figure out why. What was happening to her? Could she be developing a crush on Josh? "Frankie. It's short for Frances."

"Frankie what?"

"Baker."

Looking as if he'd just had a burst of inspiration, Josh ran over to the broadcast booth door. "You want to hear tomorrow's story?"

"You've written it already?"

"No." With an impish grin, he tapped a finger on the side of his head and stepped inside the booth.

"Don't go on the air! You'll spoil it!"

"It's after six — nobody's here except us.

42

Besides, I've only got the room monitors turned on."

The booth's light flicked on as Josh slipped inside. He sat down on the chair, looking out the window at Frankie. Putting on a set of earphones, he leaned over the mike.

Through a set of speakers hanging in the corners, his voice boomed out, smooth and confident — and so fast Frankie really had to listen to catch the words.

"Okay, it's time to put away that dang homework you haven't finished yet and get your mind off those thoughts of Virginia Beach.... We're takin' you to our favorite spot, the town that calls itself the dead center of the United States, where pretty girls outnumber prairie dogs two to one, exactly one thousand four hundred and fifty-seven miles due west of the Capitol Beltway — that's right, Raspberry Patch, U.S.A.!"

Frankie burst into applause. He was amazing. How could he have said all of that in one breath?

Now the mood changed. Josh's voice slowed down to a chatty, friendly pace, with a slight country twang.

"You could tell it was spring in Raspberry Patch. It wasn't so much the flowers, but the spring cleaning. Yessir, all you had to do was take a whiff of the morning air — and get a noseful of carpet dust. It was a time when the thoughts of farmers turned to long, wavy blades of wheat, and the thoughts of their songs to long, wavy . . . well, let's just say there was always a bit of a crowd over at Pop's Soda Fountain — and they weren't there for the soda!"

This was incredible. Frankie had never heard anyone do something like this right off the top of his head. For all his dreaming and big talk, she could tell Josh really did have a gift.

"Pop didn't work the afternoon shift, and it was just as well, to hear any of the young men talk about it. Some said he just couldn't take the heat. But the older folks knew there was another reason. After all, it was no mistake that business would suddenly pick up when he left. . . . No, after the noon whistle there was someone else behind the counter. Someone with a smile even sweeter than the ice cream she dished out all day long. Most called her the prettiest girl in Crabtree County, and you'd have to look hard to find anybody who'd argue about that. Her name? I knew you'd ask. Well, her mama named her Frances, but there was only one name carved in the minds of every red-blooded young man for a hundred miles around — and that was Frankie Baker. . . ."

Frankie felt as though somebody had just thrown a bucket of ice water in her face. What was he doing? Frankie wasn't the kind of girl that guys went for. Rox had told her that straight to her face. Josh couldn't possibly be flirting with her. But then it hit Frankie . . . he was making fun of her.

". . . Even the day the air-conditioning broke, Pop's was full. Nobody noticed the heat, as long as Frankie was there. . . ."

Frankie was so angry she wanted to cry. Josh had seemed different than the other guys — smarter, more sensitive. But he was worse, much worse. At least the others only ignored her. They didn't go out of their way to abuse her like this.

On the verge of exploding, she bolted toward the door.

Immediately the speakers behind her became silent and the door to the booth flew open. "Hey, wait!" Josh shouted. "I was just getting started."

Frankie flung herself around to face him. Her body was shaking with anger.

"How could you do this to me?" She tried as hard as she could to stay in control. "How could you be so cruel?"

"I'm sorry, Frankie, it was all in good fun!"

"Good fun? Is it good fun to ridicule someone?"

Josh's jaw hung open in shock. "I wasn't ridiculing you at all, Frankie! What did I say that — "

"No, not at all, huh? 'The prettiest girl in Crabtree County'? 'A smile sweeter than the ice cream she dished out'? What garbage!" Tears started to well up in her eyes. "I mean, I know I'm not pretty; I have to look at myself in the mirror every morning. But you didn't have to rub it in! It's bad enough knowing people laugh at me behind my back, but no one has ever done it to my face like that!"

"No, no! You're wrong!" Josh pleaded.

"Don't tell me I'm wrong. I'm not as dumb as you think. Now leave me alone! Go back to writing your stupid stories!"

Josh's face was now twisted in confusion. "Okay, Frankie, if that's what you want," he said, bewildered. "But let me tell *you* something! I've never done a story like that for anyone, but it seems like you're so insecure and so busy feeling sorry for yourself you can't even hear what I was really saying!" He started to stalk back into the office, then turned around. "I've got news for you, Frankie. If *you* don't believe in yourself, nobody else will!"

Frankie burst into tears and ran down the corridor. She had to get out of the school before anyone saw her. She ducked out the side door and into the empty quad. There, the setting sun was casting huge shadows all around. She hid in a secluded corner near the empty bike rack and sobbed and sobbed.

Everything was all wrong. Her best friend was using her like a puppet, and now, a complete stranger had humiliated her.

Or had he? Frankie didn't know what to believe. And even if he *was* telling the truth, he'd probably never talk to her again!

She took off her glasses and wiped her eyes. Well, at least there's one positive thing, she thought. I didn't have to give Roxanne's message to Greg. That didn't exactly outweigh the bad things, but it was a start. Sighing, she pulled herself together and slowly began the long walk home.

Chapter
6

"Easy there! This isn't the Olympics, you know!" Dr. Merwin held out his arms as Katie's knees wobbled beneath her.

"Look at that! It's disgusting! When am I ever going to be able to really get around again?" Katie exclaimed. She glared down at her thin, pale leg.

"You've had a little muscle loss over the past couple of months, that's all. It's only natural," Dr. Merwin said. "Give it a few more weeks of physical therapy. It'll be back to normal before you know it."

Katie limped slowly around the office. She was dying to do a running backflip, or at least a split, in the doctor's hallway. But not with *this* leg. Not for a long time, if ever. She didn't know whether to laugh or cry. The cruddy old cast was finally off for good, and she felt so light and free. Her leg looked ridiculous, though, like a rag doll's. It made her other one look positively *fat*.

"What about gymnastics, Dr. Merwin?" she asked, hoping desperately for the answer she wanted.

He shook his head. "I've got to be honest with you, Katie. It doesn't look very good. You've got to take it slowly; it's almost like learning to walk again. If the muscles don't strengthen properly around the bone, you may have some long-term problems."

Katie nodded sadly. She knew Dr. Merwin felt for her; she could see it in her eyes. "Thanks for taking such good care of me," she said softly. Grabbing her cane, she limped out of the office.

But as soon as she stepped outside, she felt a sudden rush of relief and hope. No more crutch rashes under her arms, no more itches on her leg that she couldn't reach. And the doctor hadn't said she definitely could *not* do gymnastics this year. Now she knew where she stood. It was time to get back into life again.

For the first time, she allowed herself to take a breath of the soft, warm spring air. She looked around at the shopping plaza next door. It was dark out, and the Hall of Fame seemed to be filling up. Her mouth curled into a grin as she wondered how she could have been low enough to go in there.

Well, at least no one saw me there, she thought. But walking away, Katie felt a twinge of sneaky, guilty joy. She'd done something forbidden that no one would ever know about, and that somehow pleased her.

The next day, Katie went to school feeling a

little afraid. She was scared that her bad moods had cut off her friendships, and that she'd never be able to patch things up with Greg. But even before school started, her first fear began to lift. As she struggled up the school steps, a group of four kids smiled at her from the top of the stairs: Brian, Karen, Eric, and Colin.

"It's the queen of the parallel bars, and she's walking again!" Brian exclaimed with a wide grin. The whole group stepped aside and gave Katie a round of applause.

"Lookin' good!" Colin called out.

"Good?" Karen objected. "She looks more than good. How about fantastic, amazing, incredible?"

One by one, the other students on the steps joined in the cheers. Katie barely recognized some of them.

It felt so good. For a moment — just a moment — she couldn't care less about gymnastics. The support of her classmates was all she needed.

Katie's mood stayed happy all day. It didn't hurt that Matt Jacobs said she looked beautiful during lunch period, or that Diana ran across a crowded hallway between classes just to hug her. She was beginning to feel like her old self again. For the first time all spring, she felt glad just to be alive, and hopeful that her friends hadn't given up on her.

But by the end of last period, she still hadn't faced the two people she cared about the most — her best friend Molly, and Greg.

There was still a trace of fear left as she sat in the crowd's old meeting place in the quad. It felt comforting to be in this spot, where the whole group had shared so much over the last couple of years — stories, homework, love problems. It was only a cherry tree and a couple of old benches, but everyone knew it would hold a special place in their memories long after graduation.

She settled back on a bench and took a few deep breaths, trying to quiet her nerves.

"Katie?" a soft voice called out. "Hi, mind if I sit down?"

Katie spun around. "Molly! Yes! I mean, no! I mean, sit down!"

Slowly, a little stiffly, Molly sat down on the other bench. A tense smile was on her face. She probably thinks I'm going to get mad at her about something, Katie thought. "Uh, do you like my new leg?" she finally said. She held it as high as she could and jiggled it around.

"Not bad," Molly replied, with a giggle. "Almost as good as new." She nodded.

Katie smiled and nodded, too. Molly smiled and nodded back. They both laughed nervously. The breeze blew a strand of hair across Molly's face, and she pushed it back. Then she brushed a smudge of dirt off her shoe.

Katie looked around at the trees, the benches, the school. The silence was killing her. She looked at Molly and sighed. "You know, this is ridiculous."

Molly smiled. Her dark blue eyes looked straight into Katie's. "Yeah, I was thinking the same thing."

"I'm . . . I'm really sorry, Moll. I mean, I know

I've been sort of crazy lately. I'm sorry if I took it out on you."

"Does that mean I don't have to worry about what I say in front of you anymore?"

Katie laughed. The two girls stood up and threw their arms around each other. "Oh, it's so good to see you happy again!" Molly said. "For a while there, I thought we'd lost you."

"I know," Katie answered, flashing her friend a sheepish grin as she slowly sat back down. "It's so weird. I . . . I just can't tell you what it's been like. . . ."

"Frustrating, huh?"

Katie felt her eyes welling up. "Oh, Molly, I feel so helpless . . . so *worthless*. I used to look forward to working out every day, and now I have to concentrate on just getting myself around! Molly, I miss the gym so badly. I know I just have to accept it, but. . . ."

"I know," Molly said. Sitting down next to Katie, she put a comforting hand on her friend's shoulder. "I wish I could say something that would help, but I have the feeling there isn't anything. I can help you make the best of things, though. There's lots of things we can do — go to the sub shop, go to movies, just talk . . ."

"Yeah, I guess you're right," Katie said. "I — I just haven't been feeling very friendly. I guess I'm afraid of being a big burden on everybody."

Molly put her arms around Katie and gave her a big hug. "Forget it, okay? You're stuck with me whether you like it or not."

Katie sat back. For a moment, the two of them were silent again, wrapped up in thought. "I miss

52

our talks," Katie finally said. "It feels like we haven't done this in such a long time."

Molly sighed. "I know. I feel bad about that, too. I haven't really tried to approach you because you've seemed like you needed to be left alone. I didn't want to bug you."

"Well, you did the right thing. I probably would have bitten your head off." Katie's eyes dropped downward. "Just like I did to everyone else who tried to help me."

"Like Greg?" Molly asked gently.

Katie nodded. She hardly ever cried, but this time she couldn't help it. Silent tears rolled down her cheeks.

"What happened?" Molly asked, brushing a stray hair out of Katie's face. "Is it Greg?"

"No," Katie answered. "At least, not yet. But I'm really worried." She searched Molly's eyes. "You know Greg pretty well. I want you to promise to give me an honest opinion, okay?"

"Of course!"

"Good. Just tell me, do you think there's a chance for us anymore?"

"For you and Greg?" Molly leaned back and raised her eyebrows. A wave of fear shot through Katie. "Do french fries go with hamburgers? Does peanut butter go with jelly?"

"You mean it?" Katie squeezed Molly's hand. "Oh, you are the *best* friend! Wait, you're not just saying this to make me happy, are you?"

"Are you kidding? Greg hasn't been the same since you started to drift away. No more jokes, none of that flashy wit. And he hardly ever draws cartoons anymore!"

"Seriously?" Now Katie *really* wanted to cry. What had she ever done to deserve someone as devoted as Greg?

"Katie, you should *see* his eyes light up whenever someone mentions your name! He tries to hard not to let it show, but I don't think he ever thinks of anything else!"

"Oh, I want so badly to believe that, Molly. But after the way I've been treating him, I don't know how I can face him again."

Molly put her hand on Katie's shoulder. "Its got to be done. You could go talk to him right now."

"Now?"

"Sure. I just saw him in the student council room, working on plans for the auction. I'm sure he's still there."

"I don't know. . . . Maybe I should wait a day, until I feel — "

"Come on, Katie, this is a perfect time. He's so hung up on you, he'll forget everything in a second if you just say how sorry you are."

Katie fidgeted in her seat for a minute. Just the thought of facing Greg, of seeing the hurt in his face, tore her apart. But Molly was probably right; it wouldn't get any easier. "Wh–what'll I say to him?"

A broad smile worked its way across Molly's face. "What else? Ask him to the prom!"

"What?" Katie was hoping she wouldn't choke on "Hi," let alone. . . .

"You know he'll say yes. You won't even give him a chance to be mad at you!"

Katie sat back and thought about it for a

minute. When Molly put it that way, it didn't sound like such a bad idea. "You're right, Molly, as usual," she said. "I'll do it."

"You see? I can tell you feel better already!" Molly said, grinning.

Katie leaned on her cane and pushed herself up. "Wish me luck," she said.

"You don't need it," Molly answered with a smile.

Katie gave her a half-hearted smile in return and limped across the quad.

The school had that quiet, late afternoon feeling about it. The faint smell of floor-cleaner hung in the air, and only the sound of a distant, muffled vacuum cleaner broke the eerie silence. Just past the computer room, Katie turned right. As she walked slowly down the hallway, a lump began to grow in her throat. Keep it together, Crawford, she said to herself. Just remember, he wants to make it work as much as you do.

The student council room appeared to be deserted. Katie's mood fell. She realized he'd probably gone already. All this psyching up for nothing. Listlessly, she walked up to the open door to check.

"That's amazing! It looks just like Mr. McQuame! You're *so* talented, Greg!"

Katie stopped cold. The voice was familiar, but not one that she wanted to hear.

"I *love* drawing cartoons," the voice continued, "but mine are so amateurish compared to yours. I'm telling you, if you auctioned off some portraits of the students, you'd make a bundle!"

Roxanne, Katie thought with growing anger. What is *she* doing in there?

"Maybe, but portraits really aren't my thing. I'm more into political cartoons. But I'll do them if you think it'll help get some more Stevenson students involved in the prom plans."

"Oh, Greg, I *told* you not to worry about that. It's as good as done. I've been talking to them all week, telling them how great you guys are. They've got this *ridiculous* idea that your whole group is snobby. Can you believe it?" She let out a high, lilting, *fake* laugh.

"No, I can't. We've all gone out of our way to be friendly to them," Greg said. "And Karen's interview — "

"That helped. You have to understand, though, they're a little insecure. It was tough for them to change schools. But for some reason, they listen to me. I guarantee by the end of the week, they'll all be offering to help out with the auction."

"That's fantastic, Roxanne. I don't know how I can thank you."

"Well, you've really gotten me excited about this auction, Greg. The idea is just brilliant!"

Three options ran through Katie's mind: walking away, throwing up, or cracking her cane over Roxanne's head. How could anyone be so obvious, so manipulative . . . and how could Greg be dumb enough to fall for it?

She closed her eyes and counted to ten. Molly's words floated through her mind: He'll forget everything if you say you're sorry. There was no choice. She had to do something now, before

Roxanne got her claws in any further.

Standing as straight as possible, with a nonchalant smile on her face, Katie stepped into the room.

"Sounds like there's a prom meeting going on in here," she said firmly.

"No, not today!" Roxanne sang out in a polite but annoyed voice. As she looked up to see Katie, her expression barely changed. Just a flicker of shock and frustration crossed her face. It was brief, and she stifled it instantly, but Katie still noticed.

So did Greg. He turned around, and as soon as he saw Katie his mouth dropped open. The pen he was holding clattered to the floor.

"How great," Roxanne said dully. "The cast is off — "

Without saying a word, Greg leaped out of his seat and took Katie's free hand. "Let me see," he said, looking her up and down with a huge smile. "You look terrific. How does it feel?"

Molly was right. All the love was still there, still shining in his eyes. "Fantastic, Greg. It — " She looked deeply into those incredible eyes and said exactly what was on her mind. "It feels as wonderful as you look."

Greg gave her a big hug. "Speak for yourself, K.C. It's great to see that smile again."

"Can we talk for a second, Greg?" She cast a quick glance in Roxanne's direction.

"Oh! Sure! We were just chatting about prom plans." He called over his shoulder, "Excuse us a minute, okay, Roxanne?"

Katie and Greg took a few steps into the hall-way. "I–I don't know where to begin, Greg," Katie said. "Um, I guess I came here to say I'm sorry. I know I've been rotten to you ever since — "

Greg put his finger tenderly on Katie's lips. "It's all right," he said. "You don't have to apologize. I was a little impatient with you, too, you know. Let's just forget it, okay?"

Katie nodded happily and opened her arms. In one swift motion, Greg scooped her off the ground and twirled her around.

"I knew you'd come through," he said over Katie's giggles.

"Well, as you can see, it's not over yet," she said.

"But you're having physical therapy, right?" He gently set her back down.

"Yeah. I think I'll also coach some of the younger girls on the team while I'm recovering. And, well, who knows. . . ." A sly glint formed in her eyes. "Maybe I'll be able to show them a thing or two."

"You haven't changed a bit," Greg said.

"Mmm, neither have you," Katie answered with a grin. "Listen, I'd like to help out with the prom plans. How are they going?"

"Lots of kids from Kennedy have volunteered, but zilch from Stevenson. That's what Roxanne and I were talking about. She's going to try to get all her friends involved — "

"Did I hear my name?" Roxanne called out. Katie and Greg turned to see her appear in the doorway. Her long hair looked as if it had just been brushed, and she smiled sweetly as she clung to the doorjamb.

"Guess what? Katie's going to help out with the prom plans!" Greg said.

"Oh, wonderful!" Roxanne said. She tossed her head back and looked directly into Katie's eyes. "That's funny, I thought you were usually busy after school."

Katie pointed to her leg. "Not with this, Roxanne. It kind of limits me."

"Oh. Then I guess you're going to come around on nights you're not at the Hall of Fame. That *is* the name of that place, isn't it?"

Katie felt as though her insides had just fallen out. Greg started to laugh, until he saw the expression on Katie's face. "Hey, Roxanne, that's really not very funny . . ." he said.

Roxanne shrugged her shoulders. She held up her hand and looked lazily at her red nails. "Who said it was supposed to be funny? I'm just stating a fact. It's common knowledge — everybody knows Katie hangs out there these days."

Greg's eyes widened, and he gave Katie a strange look. "But you would *never* . . . that place is *disgusting*!"

Katie's jaw was so tightly clenched, her teeth ached. She couldn't look Greg in the eye.

"No," he muttered. "I can't believe this."

It was either leave now or explode, Katie thought. How did Roxanne know? How could she have been cruel enough to bring it up in front of Greg like that?

"What's wrong?" Roxanne said innocently. "What kind of kids hang out there, anyway?"

59

"Say something, Katie," Greg pleaded. "What's going on? Is that where you were yesterday afternoon?"

But she couldn't. At least not something that she'd want him to hear. Greg was wonderful, but *so* straight and narrow. How could he ever understand this?

She looked into his eyes. They were filled with pain and searching for a denial she couldn't give.

No, there was no hope. Just before the tears began to spill down her cheeks, Katie limped away as fast as her cane could take her.

Chapter 7

"Yes, it's half-past a salami sandwich and quarter till that last cold milk shake — time for the show that made lunch period famous: *Cloaks and Jokes!*"

Josh adjusted his earphones and lifted his program notes. This was going to be a long one.

"Is that extra something missing in your life? You've trudged through more than two-thirds of the school year and the most exciting thing that happened was when your dog ate your little sister's homework last November? Well, relief is on the way! That's right, plans for the Kennedy High Spring Auction are in full gear. So save your pennies, 'cause all the proceeds are going to the prom. And what will you get in return? Just listen. . . ."

Josh quickly glanced out into the studio. As usual, his new engineer, Alex Aldrich, was monitoring the sound and hanging on to Josh's every word.

And also as usual, Brian Pierson was looking grumpily at his watch, nervous that Josh would go over his time limit again. Josh lifted the stack of notes and took a deep breath.

"Are you juniors confused about applying to colleges — so many places, so little time? Well, Holly Daniels will solve your problem! No, she's not auctioning off her scholarship to the University of Montana. But she will give expert advice to the highest bidder!

"Tired of academics? Ah, now you're listening! Bid for a spot in the Potomac River Fun Race with Greg Montgomery, or free horseback-riding lesson courtesy of Diana Einerson. And that's just the beginning. You could find instant fame as the star of Jeremy Stone's next video, buy a photographic portrait by Dee Patterson, a signed copy of the hot new mystery novel by Jonathan Preston's mother, or a singing telegram from Elise Hammond. Or you could become a martial-arts expert with aikido lessons from Molly Ramirez. You could lube those pistons — or at least learn what it means — when Matt Jacobs fixes your car!"

Josh paused and looked closely at something scribbled at the bottom of the page.

"And here's one that was just added. For those of you who think a hypotenuse is something you see at the zoo, you can bid on math tutoring from the former whiz of Stevenson High, Frankie Baker!"

The rest of the show was pretty standard stuff. Lots of news, lots of sports, and all of it boring. It was the part of the show he let Alex write, and it always seemed to take the longest to read. He was happy to get to the last section, the weather.

". . . so the update from Josh's weather watch is: put away those raincoats and umbrellas. In fact, you can put away most of your clothes for the rest of this warm week, too. But don't go too far. Let's keep it clean, folks."

He put down the stack of papers and reached for his Raspberry Patch notes. He'd been excited about the story all day. The night before he'd gotten carried away and stayed up till midnight writing it.

But somehow, as he launched into his fast-talk intro to Raspberry Patch, the story faded from his mind. He was thinking of something much more important. Something he just couldn't ignore.

He put his story notes down and looked up at the clock. Two more minutes. Josh glanced at Brian and Alex, who seemed to know something was up. They were staring at him as if he had just gone crazy.

Josh cleared his throat. He'd always been able to spin stories off the top of his head, but he'd never tried it on the air.

"It happened every year," he began. "Yes sir, the sickness had taken hold of Raspberry Patch. You could tell by the look of disgust on old Beatrice Northrop's face as she rocked on her porch opposite the high school and watched the poor victims. The signs were obvious: too much laughter in the schoolyard, outrageous acts like kissing and hugging in public. Some chalked it up to adolescent lunacy, but they were the ones who never had it. The rest of us called it spring fever."

Josh looked through the booth window. Brian's and Alex's faces were frozen in amazement. Josh began to feel all charged up inside. The words continued to flow out effortlessly.

"Now this illness seemed to strike just about everyone to some degree. But one lonely, shy boy — so shy he never told me his name — had it worst of all. And he was afraid to show it.

"The poor fella had been feeling just fine until he walked into Pop's Soda Fountain one day. But the fever struck suddenly when he took one look behind the counter. It was a girl, and even though girls had never been such a big deal to him before, this one somehow stole his heart. She was the most beautiful girl in town, he thought, but danged if he knew how to tell her that.

"Now the girl had somehow managed to avoid the fever. Some think she was too smart to get sick; after all, she was known all over as the sweetest girl of Crabtree County. But the shy boy soon figured out the real reason. You see, one day he finally told her, in his own funny way, how he felt. Now, if the truth be told, the beautiful, sweet girl was starting to feel a little feverish herself, and she was well aware that the sickness could pass from one person to another. But she knew how to stay healthy. Yessir, the secret was not to believe what the boy told her. She said he was lying, and she ordered him to go away.

"Well, the boy went home, crushed, and sicker than ever. The beautiful girl had stayed away from the illness, but somehow she looked so sad. After all, what the boy had told her was true. Maybe she was so afraid of getting a little spring fever that she just didn't believe in herself anymore.

"The boy dreamed about the girl all week long. He hoped she was dreaming about him, too, but in his heart he knew it wasn't true. He knew that a person who didn't believe in anything was a person without dreams."

Josh paused again. He'd pulled it off! Maybe now Frankie would understand how he felt. In the back of his mind, though, he also realized that this might have been the stupidest thing he'd ever done.

"This is Josh Ferguson for *Cloaks and Jokes*. We're out of time, but that's as far as the story goes anyway. I'm still looking for a way to finish it, so I invite any of my listeners to write an ending of your own. Just leave it under the door at station WKND. And now it's time for *Soundings* with Brian Pierson!"

The beat of a UB40 song started, and Josh took off his earphones. Brian rushed into the booth, and Josh gave him the seat. "Great story, but weird," Brian commented as he adjusted the mike.

Josh smiled and left the booth. "How did you memorize that?" Alex asked. "You didn't even look at your notes!"

A voice from behind them answered, "Genius, Alex. That's the only word for it."

They turned to see Karen standing in the doorway.

"Oh, come on, Karen, it was just a dumb little story," Josh countered with an impish smile.

In a voice that was meant to sound like Josh, Karen said, "She tried to compliment him, but he wouldn't believe it. Maybe — "

"Okay, Okay," Josh said, laughing. "It was brilliant, I admit it!"

"That sounds more like the Josh I know! Listen, I have some good news," she added. "Can Brian talk?"

"He's just put on a couple of tunes," Alex called out. "I can tell him to come out."

"Great. This will only take a minute."

She sat down and opened her shoulder bag as Brian stepped out of the booth. "Hi! I thought you'd be working up in the newspaper office. What's up?"

Karen took out a stack of papers and put them on the table. "Letters to the editor," she announced. "All of them are complimenting my interview with Lily Rorshack."

Josh picked one up and read it:

"I never really read that much in The Red and the Gold *until the last issue. I was at the last forensics meet and saw Lily Rorshack win the humorous improv contest, so I picked up the interview out of curiosity. Well, it was so fantastic I read it three times. Who would have thought that somebody so smart and funny had such a tough life, living on the street and getting busted? Congratulations on an article so good it puts the* Washington Post *to shame!"*

"Whoa! Tell me you didn't write this yourself, Karen!"

"That's fantastic," Brian said, giving her a hug. "This article's probably good enough to win you a spot on the Brown newspaper next year!"

"That would be nice," Karen agreed, "but I don't think it works that way. Nobody hears about a high school newspaper article, anyway. Unless it wins some kind of national award or something."

"Listen to this one!" Josh called out.

> *"This is the most inspirational article I've ever read. My parents both cried when they read it, and they're sending copies to other schools so other families who are having similar problems can get help. They're sure it will make a difference."*

Karen beamed. "I can hardly believe it! And to think, I almost didn't meet Lily. Remember, Brian? We thought a student interview would be too dull! Now I'm so glad I listened to Daniel."

"Daniel who?" Josh asked.

"Daniel Tackett, some pushy twerp from Stevenson," Brian answered. "He was the editor-in-chief of the *Stevenson Sentinel*, and he came into *The Red and the Gold* office trying to prove how superior his paper was — "

"Oh, don't be so sour, Brian. First of all, he made some good points," Karen said. "And he is the one who arranged the interview with Lily. I think maybe he was trying in his own way to help bring the two schools together."

"Maybe . . ." Brian answered. "But I still think he's trouble."

Just then Alex called out, "Thirty seconds!"

"See you in a minute," Brian said and went back into the booth.

Josh was getting a kick out of the letters. He could just imagine what each person's voice sounded like from the things they wrote. "You ought to save these," he told Karen. "Someday when you're a Pulitzer Prize winning journalist you'll be able to look back at them."

Karen laughed. "You live in a dream world, Josh! Sometimes I think you have Raspberry Patch on the brain."

"I'm serious! Have you thought of submitting this article to the *Post*?"

"Forget it. I know someone who tried that once. She submitted a huge feature article that had won first prize in a regional competition. Everyone thought the *Post* would eat it up. She waited six months and got a form letter rejecting the article. They even spelled her name wrong! The papers don't want to be bothered with articles by high school kids!"

"It just seems like such a shame no one outside Kennedy will get a chance to read this."

"Maybe, but I missed the deadline for the National Scholastic Press Competition by two weeks."

Suddenly an idea hit Josh. "What about the Georgetown Competition?" he said. "That's going on right now!"

"What? How do you know?"

"Hey, I know all *kinds* of trivial stuff. I read loads of newspapers every day — you know, to get ideas for the show. I remember coming across something about a journalism contest at Georgetown University. Professors from all these big East Coast colleges are judging the articles. I think it was in Tuesday's paper."

"Come on, Josh. I know this article's a big deal in Rose Hill, but —"

"Just think of how many people it could help! Not to mention the publicity! I mean, how would winning first prize look on your resume when you try out for the Brown paper?"

Josh could tell Karen was softening. He sat back and let her think.

Brian's voice crackled over the speakers:

"And that was The Clangers, who will be seen in person at Kennedy High — providing enough money can be raised at our auction! Okay, our next song is by a group that's starting to hit big in the New York clubs. Here's They Might Be Giants!"

As the music started, Brian came out of the booth again. He gave Karen a puzzled look. "Is something wrong?"

"Brian," she said, adjusting her red plastic-framed glasses, "I need your advice."

Brian looked from Karen to Josh. "What's up? What kind of crazy ideas is Josh putting in your head?"

"Josh found out about this journalism competition that Georgetown University is sponsoring. Do you think I should enter the interview in it?"

"Sure, why not?"

"Well, it sounds like a big deal, and there'll be all these big professors judging it, and I don't know . . . I mean, all the hotshot writers from the best high schools enter these things, kids who

70

have summer jobs with real newspapers. And the prizes always go to political articles. . . ."

"You *are* one of those hotshots, Karen!" Josh blurted out.

". . . and after all," Karen went on, "it *is* someone else's life. What if it would embarrass Lily?"

"It sounds to me like you're trying to talk yourself out of it," Brian said.

"I guess maybe I am. Maybe I shouldn't be so negative. I mean, the topic *is* really interesting. . . ."

"Not to mention the writing!" Josh couldn't understand why Karen was so reluctant.

"Look," said Brian. "It's really up to you. I think you should do whatever makes you feel comfortable." He went over to the table to put away some cassettes.

Josh hopped up from his seat. "Karen, the only thing keeping you back is fear! Your article is wonderful — I could *never* write something as sensitive as that. Besides, what's the worst that could happen? You lose, you get a nice thank-you letter. But who knows, you might blow them away! How many stories like this are there in a suburban high school?"

Karen's brow was furrowed. Josh *knew* she really wanted that article to go somewhere.

He gently touched her hand and waited until she looked him in the eye. "Let's face it," he continued. "It would be selfish *not* to do it, Karen. Think of the people who won't be helped because they didn't even get a chance to read the article."

Karen nodded solemnly. She gathered up all her letters and put them back in her bag.

71

"You're right," she said. "Win or lose, I really want people to read this."

"Great!" Josh shouted. "I'll bring in the address tomorrow." There was no doubt in his mind — Karen's interview with Lily Rorshack was going to create a sensation!

Chapter
8

"So what special qualities may we conclude belong to a hyperbola which is asymptotic to the xy axes?"

Frankie's head was spinning. For the first time all semester, she had absolutely no interest in what Ms. Cathcart was saying. Math was the furthest thing from her mind. All she could think about was how many minutes there were until school was over — and each one seemed like three years.

"No answers?" Ms. Cathcart continued. "I'm surprised! This one should be perfectly, uh, perfectly obvious."

What is this fluttering feeling? Frankie thought, trying to relax. I wonder if it's dangerous. Maybe I'm having a heart attack. She could practically see her heart beating under her blouse. A strange prickly sensation danced around her body — first her lips, then her earlobes, then her whole scalp.

"Bill? No, hmm. Er, how about you, Charlotte? No idea . . . ? Ah well, at least I'm sure *one* of you has done your work. All right then, tell them the correct answer, please, Frankie."

Frankie. Suddenly the sound of her name didn't seem so strange, so ugly anymore. . . .

"Frankie? You *do* know the answer, don't you?"

Two more minutes to the end of class, Frankie thought. Why does everything seem so quiet all of a sudden?

"Hello? Earth to Frankie. . . ."

Frankie suddenly realized someone was talking to her. She gasped and looked around. Everyone was staring right at her. She could feel the blood rushing to her face. The snickering grew louder as students covered their mouths and looked away. It looked as if her worst nightmare had come true — the whole class was making fun of her. And the worst part of it was Ms. Cathcart was laughing, too!

"Oh, it must be spring!" Ms. Cathcart said. "Even my best students have spring fever!"

The bell rang just then, ending the torture. Frankie felt a little shaky as she stood up. She realized she must have been totally spaced-out in class. But there was no time to think of that now. She had to get to a mirror.

She plunged right into the throng of people rushing through the door. She had at least half an hour to go, but she wanted to make sure everything was absolutely right. For Zack.

She sprinted down the hallway, dodging people left and right. Oh, why did he have to do this today? she wondered for the millionth time. He could have at least given me a little more warning. I didn't even blow-dry my hair this morning!

She darted into the girls' room and let the door slam behind her. She looked around and breathed a sigh of relief. It was totally empty. Carefully she pulled a folded-up piece of spiral notebook paper out of her bag. She wanted to take a picture of the note in her mind, to memorize the way the letters went, the way the big *Z* cut across the bottom of the page. She repeated it softly to herself as she read:

Hey Franko,
Please meet me at 4:30 near the track. There's something about the prom I need to ask you. It's really important. Nod if you can come.
Zack

Frankie had blushed and nodded. That nod must have been so small, but when she did it, it had felt as if her head were the size of the whole classroom. Maybe there still *was* a chance for the two of them . . . after that whole mess with Holly, maybe Zack has finally seen how crazy Frankie was about him. She looked over the note one last time. Never would she ever forget those words.

She looked in the mirror. Her hair was a little limp, but for some reason, she didn't look as bad as she thought. She smiled. If she pulled back the right side of her mouth just enough, there was even sort of a dimple; she'd have to remember that. Maybe Josh is right, she thought. She'd heard his show at lunchtime that day and listened to every word. It had made her furious; everyone in the whole cafeteria was probably staring at her. If she hadn't been so embarrassed, she would have marched over to WKND and demanded that he retract his show. But now she realized that he might have really been complimenting her. Maybe she *wasn't* as goony-looking as she thought. After all, Zachary McGraw wanted to meet her . . . to talk about the *prom*.

The prom. Suddenly Frankie realized she hadn't thought of what she would wear. Didn't some girls get their dresses way in advance? Wasn't it a good idea to shop around a lot, maybe even have one made just for you?

So many things raced through her mind, but she couldn't think of them all now. She had to do something about her hair.

Quickly, she took out a brush. But no matter how much she stroked, her hair still hung down, all thin and stringy. She searched through her knapsack for a barrette. Panic began to set in. Purse, pens, a calculator, gum, a scarf . . . no barrette.

She took out the scarf. It was the pretty orange one her mother had given her for her birthday. She rolled it up and used it to tie her hair back.

There. That looks kind of cute, she thought. I just wish I had some makeup. Just then she remembered something she'd seen on TV once. She looked in the mirror and pinched her cheeks a few times. A little red color began to form. Well, it's not blush, but it'll have to do.

She turned to leave, but just before she reached for the door handle, she remembered one last thing — her glasses. Yanking them off, she stepped into the hallway.

Her heart was still pounding as she slowly walked toward the exit nearest the track, trying not to bounce too much. Roxanne always told her she bounced when she walked, and it made her look like a boy.

Some of the Kennedy kids were gathered on the benches in the quad. She wanted to wave but couldn't make out their faces. Walking briskly away from them, she vowed to get contact lenses.

Way off behind the school, she could vaguely see the oval shape of the track. She checked her watch. Four twenty. Ten minutes to kill. She leaned up against a fence.

She didn't want to go over there just yet; Zack might get scared away if he thought she seemed too eager. Opening up a computer program manual, she pretended to study, but of course, she couldn't read a word.

By the time one minute had passed, she'd already looked at her watch four times. She could barely hold her book still. It was as if the butterflies in her stomach had started to fly into her arms and legs, too. I can't face him in this state, she thought. Maybe I should just go home. . . .

"Hi! You're early! Why didn't you come over? Didn't you see me waving at you?"

Frankie's head jerked up at the sound of the voice. She almost dropped her book. There, running toward her with long, graceful strides, was Zack.

"Oh! No, sorry, I, uh . . . I must have been looking in the other direction."

He's gorgeous. That was the only thought in her mind just then. She may not have had her glasses on, but some things were easy to see. His Kennedy track team sweatshirt had cut-off sleeves, revealing his beautiful, lean arms. And the muscles in his legs rippled gently as he slowed down and stopped. She tried not to stare.

"No problem," he said with a smile that made Frankie melt. "Listen, this is a short break so I can't really talk that long. I had to ask you something. You're the only one I could ask."

Frankie hoped he didn't notice her gulp. It felt as though she'd swallowed a horse. Her heart pounded so loud she thought it could be heard across the courtyard. She tried to sound nonchalant. "Sure, Zack, what is it?"

Frankie could feel her face starting to turn red in anticipation. She wished she could have a videotape of this moment, but she also knew she'd remember it forever anyway.

"I . . . I feel really funny asking you this, but . . ." he stammered.

It was all she could do to keep from screaming *yes*! before he finished.

". . . I really need your advice."

All Frankie's rushing thoughts stopped short. That wasn't what was supposed to come out of his mouth. "Huh?"

"Well, you always seem to know the right answers. I can never think these things out straight." He shifted from foot to foot, and stared at the ground. "I really want to ask Holly Daniels to the prom, but. . . ."

Frankie felt as though someone had just punched her in the stomach. She leaned against the fence for support.

Zack must have noticed something because he suddenly broke off speaking and looked at her. "Oh, I know," he rushed on, with a guilty smile, "you must be so sick of me asking you about Holly. And I even know what you're going to say: She's still hung up on Bart. But I was thinking, he *is* away at college, and Holly might feel bad if no one at least asks her to the prom, right? I mean, *you'd* feel bad, wouldn't you?"

Frankie felt numb all over. Her books pulled on her arms like lead weights. How stupid of me to get so worked up, she thought. I should have known. It's happened so many times before and it's happened again. When am I ever going to learn? "I guess she would," Frankie said. She took a deep breath, trying not to cry. "I mean, *any* girl would!" She couldn't believe she'd said it. Now he'd know for *sure* what was on her mind. He'd never want to speak to her again.

"It's not like I want to steal her away from Bart or anything. I just want to be her friend, you know what I mean?"

She forced herself to answer. "Why . . . why don't you just tell her that?"

"You mean ask her, but not really *ask her*?"

Frankie nodded.

Zack's face slowly lit up. "Yeah," he said, "that makes a lot of sense. It's so simple!" He beamed at her. "I'll just say that I'm asking her as a friend, so she won't feel left out!"

Frankie tried as hard as she could to smile.

"You're a genius!" Zack continued. "Thank you!" He gave a little skip and turned to go. Her shoulders slumped forward, Frankie started to walk away.

"Oh, wait!" Zack called out. He looked over as he ran back toward her. "I heard about you auctioning your tutoring over the loudspeakers today at lunch. Guess what?"

"What?"

"I'm going to put in a bid for it!"

"You are?" All of a sudden, new hope rushed through her. Maybe he really does like me, she thought. Maybe this is just his way of saying it. I mean, he knows I'll tutor him anyway — he doesn't have to bid for it. Her heart started beating faster again. That's it. He had to break the ice by talking about Holly.

"That's right," he answered. "And I'm going to get it, if I have to bid all afternoon!"

"Great!" Frankie said. "Probably everyone else will be bidding for the more fun things. I don't think you'll have too much competition!"

Zack laughed and gave a happy little punch in the air. "There better not be! I'm about to flunk geometry!" With that, he jogged off.

For a long moment, Frankie just stood there. Passing geometry, she said to herself. That's all he's worried about. She pulled the scarf out of her hair and put it in her bag. Then she reached for her glasses and put them on again. He didn't even say anything about the way she looked, she thought. He couldn't care less. Who was she trying to kid? Slowly she walked out of the quad.

Frankie had never felt this foolish before. It was as if someone had knocked her down, picked her up, and then whacked her in the face.

As she got farther away from the school, a feeling of anger began to build. She was angry at Josh Ferguson for his ridiculous story, for trying to turn her into the same kind of stupid dreamer he was. She vowed she would never forgive him for making her feel worse than she'd ever felt in her life.

Chapter
9

The final bell rang and Katie hopped up from her desk.

"YEEEEOOOOUCH!" she screamed. Her leg buckled beneath her, and she clutched the desk in pain.

"Are you all right?" someone called out. Katie glanced around to see about six students gathered by her desk.

"I'm fine," she answered through clenched teeth. It was about the fifth time she'd done something like that this week. Katie kept forgetting her leg wasn't back to normal.

She'd gotten her cast off a week and a half ago, but every day things seemed to be getting worse and worse. Oh, her leg *was* getting better — Dr. Merwin had told her the physical therapy was working wonders. What was harder and harder to bear was waking up in the morning after a dream of an Olympic medal, and eagerly jumping out of bed, only to crumple to the floor. It was thinking of gymnastics practice as soon as the final bell rang, only to remember she couldn't do anything but sit on the sidelines.

Not to mention the looks of pity she got in the hallways every day, even from people she didn't know.

Katie forced a smile. "Really, you guys go ahead," she said at last. "I'm fine, honest. No big deal."

As everyone left the room, she slowly got up. Perfect timing, Crawford, she said to herself. Screw up your leg on a physical therapy day. She could just see Dr. Merwin shaking his head and warning her to stay away from gymnastics until the fall.

She limped down the hallway to her locker. All along the walls were brightly colored signs that read:

GOT THE CASH? WE'VE GOT THE LOOT!
BID 'EM UP
AT THE FIRST ANNUAL KENNEDY HIGH AUCTION!
AND HELP BRING THE CLANGERS
* D.C.'S HOTTEST NEW GROUP *
TO THE PROM!
APRIL 30 IN THE AUDITORIUM
IMMEDIATELY AFTER SCHOOL

She tried to feel excited about the auction, but it was impossible. Every time she saw the sign, every time someone mentioned it, it just reminded her of Greg. She couldn't get the look of scorn on his face when he found out about the Hall of

83

Fame out of her mind. He acted as if she'd *betrayed* him or something. At first she'd just been embarrassed — and angry at Roxanne, of course. But now she was beginning to think Greg was being ridiculous. After all, what was the big deal? It was only a club, and she'd been there just twice. Even so, Greg didn't seem to want to speak to her anymore.

Katie reached her locker and yanked it open. A pile of books went crashing to the floor.

"I'll get them, Katie!" Holly Daniels called out.

"No!" Katie snapped. "I can do it!"

Holly backed off. "Okay. I, uh, I just didn't know if you might want some help."

"Uh-uh," Katie mumbled, shaking her head.

"You know, if I'd broken my leg, I'd probably be having people carry me around. You're incredible."

A flicker of a smile flashed across Katie's face. "I'm sorry I snapped, Holly. I just feel so . . . so trapped. Like this leg doesn't belong to me."

"Well, why don't you do something nonathletic for a while, to take your mind off it?"

"Like what? I'm not a good writer. I don't play a musical instrument well enough — "

"There's plenty of work to do on the auction! Why don't you come with me to the meeting? Greg's probably there now. . . ."

Holly's voice trailed off. She looked embarrassed. Katie turned away and picked up her books from the floor. Great, she thought, now Holly suspects something's wrong.

"No," Katie said, "I think I may go hang out

with the team. You know, a little coaching, give pointers to the freshmen. . . ."

Holly nodded eagerly, seeming relieved. "Right. That makes sense. Well, see you tomorrow!" she said, and headed down the hall.

Katie sighed. She was getting a little sick of hearing about that dumb auction. Everyone was making such a big deal over it, as if there were nothing else to talk about. And Greg was the worst of all. Somehow she'd never really noticed how rah-rah he was. Or maybe she had, but it didn't seem to matter before. All of a sudden his all-American spirit seemed so corny it was almost obnoxious. There he was, practically jumping for joy when Roxanne volunteered to help out — and then he turned around and treated his own girl-friend like garbage just because of a couple of harmless trips to a local dive!

She slammed her locker shut. Maybe she'd been wrong about him all along, Katie thought. Let Greg have his dumb little auction. Let him have Roxanne, too. They deserve each other! Glowering, she limped out of school.

"I'm sorry, we're really backed up today, and you're a little early. I don't think the physical therapist will be able to see you for about a half hour. You can wait if you want. . . ."

"I'll wait," Katie said. The receptionist smiled and looked back at her appointment book. Katie slumped down on a brown vinyl sofa and leafed through the magazines. *Highlights for Children. Better Homes and Gardens. Modern Maturity.*

Field and Stream. Popular Mechanics. Katie rolled her eyes; she always forgot how terrible the selection was here. It looked like it was going to be another one of those boring waits. She pulled open her shoulder bag and took out her notebook and her social studies text. At least she'd be able to get some homework done.

Her eyes wandered aimlessly across the page. She just couldn't seem to care enough about the reading assignment to actually read it. It seemed so pointless to study the customs of some country she'd probably never see.

She put the book down. Looking around, she realized that *everything* was pointless. What was the use of physical therapy anyway? she thought. Even if her leg was fine, it was already too late to even think about the league title. And what did that leave her with? Boring schoolwork and a boyfriend who would rather hang around with a sexy, conniving redhead.

Katie couldn't bear to sit still for the next half-hour. She just wanted to give up on everything, to run away. . . .

And that's when she first noticed the pounding noise.

She listened for a moment. It seemed to be coming from outside. At once she knew what it was. She smiled. It was music, coming from the Hall of Fame.

She couldn't help tapping her feet. It was weird to think that little hole-in-the-wall made some people so uneasy, like Greg, for instance. To think that her crowd was so superior. . . .

And in a flash, it dawned on Katie why she'd gone there in the first place. The kids there were just like she was — regular. Not rah-rahs like Greg. So what if they liked to have a good time. Why *not* just hang out and party? After all, was being happy any less meaningful than European history — or gymnastics, for that matter? Katie suddenly realized the Hall of Fame wasn't such a terrible place after all. In fact, it was exactly where she wanted to be.

She looked at the clock. The therapist wouldn't be free for at least twenty-five minutes. She began to get up out of her seat, but a lingering thought stopped her: Maybe going to the Hall of Fame wasn't the smartest thing to do. Things were bad enough with Greg. . . .

Wait a minute, she thought. Who cares what Greg thinks? He's not interested in me anymore, anyway. Let Roxanne be the one who worries about doing the right thing for His Highness. I'm going to do what's right for me!

Leaving her books in the waiting room, she walked outside.

The air was filled with the sharp smell of exhaust fumes as Katie approached the Hall of Fame. Right outside the club, four guys were revving up motorcycle engines while their girlfriends watched. The noise was like a chorus of machine guns, and Katie didn't know whether to hold her nose or her ears.

She smiled and walked past them. One of the guys called out, "Hey, you're the one with the crutches, right?"

Katie nodded.

The guy broke into a wide grin and pointed to her leg. "Lookin' good!"

Two of the other guys saw her, too, and gave little yells:

"Yeah!"

"All ri-i-ight!"

"Thank you," Katie said stiffly and walked past them. She felt sort of flattered. They looked so creepy, but at least they seemed pretty nice. At least they weren't wearing loafers or talking about some student council meeting, she thought.

As she walked through the front door, a heavy-metal song was practically shaking the floor. She squeezed through a crowd of people, bought some potato chips and a diet soda at the counter, and found an empty booth. Sitting at the end of the bench, she propped up her leg and gazed lazily around her.

She smiled to herself. It felt great to be in a place where nobody knew your name and nobody cared. She could just blend into the woodwork. . . .

After only a few moments, Katie realized she was being watched. Out of the corner of her eye, she could make out the figure of a dark, thin guy in a black denim jacket. He was alone in another booth, sitting absolutely still and looking over at her with piercing brown eyes.

Katie fidgeted in her seat. She looked around to see if there was another empty table farther away.

Before she could move, though, she noticed he was getting up. She glanced over and saw him put out his cigarette. Then he walked over to her.

Katie sat up straight and looked at her watch

as he loomed over her. She slid to the end of the bench to get up.

"You're not leaving, are you?" the guy said.

Katie looked up at him. Up close, she recognized him — it was the guy who had helped her up the time she'd slipped. Only he was a lot handsomer — and younger — than she'd remembered. Not gorgeous, like Greg, but attractive in a strange, offbeat way. His short, spiky black hair was brushed back in a severe style, making his dark eyes look almost fearsome. But his smile was surprisingly warm, and sharp dimples creased his smooth, rosy cheeks. He couldn't have been more than a sophomore, Katie thought. Just a kid.

"See, I have an appointment — "

"What time's the appointment?" he said, sitting down across from her.

Katie couldn't believe how insistent he was. She felt like just walking away, but something about him made her want to stick around. "In about fifteen minutes," she admitted.

"That's plenty of time. You only have to go across the parking lot."

"I know, but. . . . Wait a minute, how did you know that?"

The boy flashed a confident grin and leaned back in the seat. "Remember I saw you here a couple of weeks ago? Well, you had a cast on then, and now you don't. But you're still limping — "

"No kidding. So?"

"So?" he repeated, in an imitation of her voice. "Believe it or not, I know how to read, and the sign in front of that building over there says Rose Hill Medical Arts Center." He shrugged and propped up his feet on the table. "Someone like you would never come in unless you were in the mall for some other reason . . . like a doctor's appointment."

Katie just stared at him. He was obnoxious and cocky, but there was something that drew her to him, something exciting about his attitude. He didn't seem to care what anyone thought of him. "Aren't you going to introduce yourself?" she asked.

"Oh, pardon me!" he said in an exaggeratedly formal voice. "I *am* forgetting my manners. Hi, I'm Torrey Easton."

Katie rolled her eyes and groaned. "Easton? Don't tell me you're related to Roxanne!"

"It's not my fault!" he said quickly. "I can prove the doctor got her mixed up in the hospital with the daughter of Godzilla and the Wicked Witch of the East. By the time my mother realized they'd given her the wrong baby, it was too late."

Katie chuckled. "Is that any way to talk about your sister?"

"I was being nice. Don't get me started on her bad points."

This guy's all right, Katie thought. At least we're on the same wavelength about Roxanne. "By the way, I'm Katie Crawford," she said. "I know your sister."

"I can see you're one of her many fans, huh?" Torrey said.

"Well. . . ." Katie felt funny about saying anything bad about someone's sister.

"Go ahead," he urged. "You're not going to hurt *my* feelings."

Katie sighed. "To tell you the truth, she *has* been a little. . . ."

"Pushy and insensitive? I know," Torrey said. "She's going around trying to get the goody-goody crowd on her side. There's a bunch of preppy types she's decided to sink her fangs into. You probably even know them. . . ."

He doesn't know how true that is, she thought. "Yeah, Roxanne is getting involved with all the prom plans. Says she's wants to get the two schools to come together."

"Right," Torrey said, shaking his head in disgust. "All she wants is to wrap as many of those little mama's boys around her finger as possible before they go off to some Ivy League college and learn to become rich, boring lawyers."

Katie had never heard it put like that, but it made sense. "I guess so . . ." she said.

"You *guess* so? Katie, those school-spirit types are all the same — busy with all their little *activities*, always sticking together and turning up their noses at anyone who's different. All they care about is getting into college — and they'll step over you, Roxanne, and anybody else who gets in the way. And for what? All they're going to get is the exact same stupid life as their parents! I mean, put me to sleep, right?"

"I was like that, too, you know. I was on the gymnastics team. . . ."

"Right." He pointed to her leg. "And they really care about you now, don't they?" Suddenly he put on a sickly sweet smile. "Oh, goodness,

Katie," he said, clasping and unclasping his hands. "It looks like you won't be able to participate in our greatest-ever season. Gee, that means I'll move up a notch in the rankings! Tee-hee, I guess Muffy will have to take your picture for the Handicapped section of the yearbook! Ooh, here comes Brad! He's so cute!"

Torrey then changed personalities. He furrowed his brow and held up his chin in a heroic expression. In a deep voice he said, "Pardon me, Muffy. Does my hair look all right? I've got two point three minutes till the meeting for the Super Colossal Junior-Senior Auction. Then I'm going to write about it for the newspaper while I announce it over WDORK radio station, just before my Harvard interview. Gotta go, see you at the pep rally. Har-har!"

Katie broke out laughing. "You're crazy!" she cried.

Torrey smiled, looking pleased with himself. "Those idiots drive me crazy with their activities, their — "

"Your sister's in on that auction, you know."

"Really? No kidding!" Torrey's eyes widened. "In that case, I can't wait to go!"

"Are you serious?" Katie asked. "But you just said — "

"Not to bid!" A sly grin spread across Torreys' face. "But think what a blast it would be to sit back there and make fun of all those snobs and their stupid prom."

Katie thought about it for a minute. The whole idea of going to the auction alone made her really depressed. Having Torrey around to joke with might be kind of fun. . . .

"Want to come along?" he asked with a dark, winning smile. "Come on. No one'll even notice us. We'll sit in the back."

Katie looked at him. He made his campus hero face again and said, "It's your school *duty*, Katie!"

They both laughed. "Okay," Katie said. "Why not?"

"Great!" Torrey's expression suddenly became more serious. "Uh . . . I don't have a watch, but something tells me you're missing your appointment."

Katie looked at her watch. She was five minutes late. "They'll get over it," she said with a shrug. She got up from the table. "See you at the auction, Torrey."

He nodded good-bye as Katie turned and walked slowly out of the club. She hadn't had such a good time in ages.

Chapter
10

"What do you mean the banner isn't here? The auction's supposed to start in twenty minutes!" Greg said. He felt as if he were going to explode. How could so many things go wrong at the last minute? Before, Greg had always felt one step ahead of the game. He had prided himself on his ability to function under pressure . . . until today. Now it seemed as though the whole auction was one giant catastrophe.

"I just called the cleaners. They said they thought you wanted it tomorrow!" Holly explained.

"Tomorrow's Saturday! How could they — "

"Don't worry. They said it'll be ready in time. I'm going over to pick it up in a few minutes."

Greg sighed and went over to find the auction list. It had disappeared off the table. Looking around, he saw that Colin, Karen, and Brian each had different pages of it. Around them, students he hardly knew were practically shouting to get their attention. The frantic voices overlapped, each one saying something Greg didn't want to hear:

"My father says he can't arrange the museum tour, so scratch my name from the list. . . ."

"Yes, but I can only repair certain kinds. Should I write them down . . . ?"

"If they want to use the Nautilus machines, they have to pay the club extra. . . ."

"I've decided I want to keep the comics collection. . . ."

This is a madhouse! Greg thought. Couldn't these people have thought of this stuff beforehand? But there was no time to worry about that now. Too many other things needed doing. Greg left the student council room to check on the auditorium.

Already the main hallway was filled up with students waiting to be let in. Greg ducked down another hallway and went in one of the side entrances. Inside, the prom committee's faculty adviser was dragging the lectern to the center of the stage.

"Hi, Mr. Rizzo," Greg called out. "Here, let me help."

Together they moved it into place, and Mr. Rizzo hooked up the mike.

Greg spoke into it. "Testing, one, two, three. . . ."

"You're all ready to go!" Mr. Rizzo answered.

"That's what you think."

"Uh-oh. Sounds like trouble. You want me to hold the doors a few more minutes?"

Greg looked at his watch. "Give me another five or so . . . until I bring in the banner."

"Roger!"

"No . . . Greg," Greg said with an impish smile. He wasn't sure Mr. Rizzo caught the joke, but there was no time to stick around and find out. They really had to start moving now.

By the time he got back to the student council room, most of the frantic students were gone. Karen and Brian were scribbling furiously on clean pieces of loose-leaf paper. Colin rushed over to Greg. "Everything set up?"

"T minus about four and counting," Greg answered. "Did you straighten out all the late changes?"

"I think so. We're just copying them over so they'll be legible."

Just then Holly burst into the room with a bundle in her arms. "Hot off the presses!" she said with a little giggle. "They did a terrific job."

"Excellent! Thanks, Holly, you saved us!" Greg said. Then he called to the others, "Are we ready?"

Karen and Brian quickly finished writing, and Karen gathered up the sheets, while Brian picked up a cardboard box full of programs. Colin took another box that contained visual aids for the auction items. "We're ready," Colin said.

"Then let's go for it!" Greg shouted.

They all cheered and marched down the hallway and into the auditorium. Brian and Karen hung the banner on the stage, while Holly and Colin went to the back of the auditorium with the programs. When everything was in place, Greg gave the signal.

The doors opened to a throng of students, who filled the auditorium almost instantly. Greg was thrilled; the promotion campaign had worked! He turned to Holly, who had a huge grin on her face. Behind her, Mr. Rizzo gave the thumbs-up sign. Holly and Greg then set up five folding chairs behind the lectern, and they all sat down. Greg noticed Colin was shaking.

"It's . . . it's all so *big*!" Colin said to him. "I'm glad you're the one who has to face them — I'd pass out!"

Greg's eyes wandered over the boisterous crowd. Everyone was laughing and chatting excitedly, obviously expecting to have a good time. All the familiar faces were there, too — Dee, Marc, Jeremy, Diana, Jonathan, Matt, Molly — as well as some kids he'd only seen in the hallway.

But the thing that made him happiest was the crowd of Stevenson students. There were lots of them, sitting front and center in the auditorium. Best of all, they were talking with the Kennedy kids as if they'd been friends for years. And right smack in the middle of them was Roxanne. She seemed to be waiting for Greg's glance, and gave him a sexy wink. He smiled back. She really came through, he thought. At first he'd had a hard time taking her promise seriously, but it was clear she'd been true to her word.

Mr. Rizzo stepped up to the lectern. "Think you can handle 'em, Greg?" he said, away from the mike.

Greg laughed. "Just watch me."

He stood politely to the side as Mr. Rizzo made a few opening remarks.

"I don't think anyone up here dreamed what a turnout we'd have tonight," he began. "And I'm sure I speak for Greg, Colin, Karen, and the rest of the organizers when I say that this is going to be the best prom in the history of Kennedy High School!"

A big roar went up from the crowd. Greg punched his fist in the air and joined the cheering. He could see there were only a few seats left in the place, and people were still filing in. Just as the cheering died down, he heard a loud "Yeah, Kennedy!" way in the back. He squinted and saw a tough-looking kid in a black denim jacket bounding through the door, followed by a girl who was giggling. This is amazing, Greg thought, even the leather-and-chains gang is turning up.

As Mr. Rizzo continued his remarks, Greg couldn't help watching the two newcomers as they went to their seats in the last row. He couldn't really see the girl's face, but she didn't look as if she belonged with the guy. Her outfit was too straight. In fact, with her long red hair, she looked like *Katie*, of all people.

". . . I know you're all anxious for the fun to start," Mr. Rizzo continued, "so I'm going to hand the mike over to one of the students who has worked the hardest on the auction. I'm sure most of you know him — Greg Montgomery!"

Once again, the crowd burst into applause. A few scattered chants of "Greg! Greg!" went up.

But Greg didn't hear them. Instead, he felt an

icy chill running through his body. There was no doubt about it — that *was* Katie sitting way in the back.

For a moment he didn't know what to do. He felt like running to the back of the auditorium and finding out what was going on. But that would have ruined everything, all his hard work. He'd just have to deal with Katie later. Taking a deep breath, he smiled and began the auction.

Katie had expected the crowd to yell, but the "Yeah, Kennedy!" seemed so out of place coming from Torrey that she couldn't help laughing. As they settled into their seats, Torrey let out a loud yawn. "Whoops! Pardon me," he said, as a few students gave him dirty looks. "I couldn't sleep last night just thinking about the auction!"

"Shh," Katie said, with a guilty little smile on her face.

"So that's the guy you used to like?" Torrey asked, nodding toward the stage.

"Yeah," Katie said shyly, gazing at Greg. He looked so tall and strong on the stage. His friendly personality seemed to radiate all the way to the back.

"Mmm-hmm. He *is* a hunk," Torrey said in an effeminate voice. A brawny, athletic-looking guy in front of him spun around and stared. Torrey nudged him in the shoulder and laughed. Thinking he was being let in on a joke, the guy let out a confused laugh and turned back around.

"Me play football. Me eat beer bottles for breakfast!" Torrey muttered to Katie.

Katie tried to stifle a laugh. "You're impossible!" she said.

They watched as Greg began the auction. "How does this work?" Torrey asked.

"Look on the back of your program. There's a huge number in black magic marker. Everyone's number is different. If you want to make a bid for something, you hold the number up. That way they can keep track of who won what."

Greg's voice rang out over the loudspeaker. "Okay, what do I hear for a singing telegram from Elise Hammond? Do I hear five dollars?"

Torrey leaned toward Katie. "I think I'll hold out for something a little more exciting — like a year's supply of dental floss."

Immediately someone put a hand up, holding out their program.

"How about six?" Greg said.

Someone else raised a program.

"Seven!" another person yelled.

"Nine!"

"Nine-fifty!"

The highest bid is nine-fifty!" Greg said. "Anybody want to go higher . . . ? Do I hear ten . . . ? Someday you'll be paying a lot more than nine-fifty to hear *this* voice . . . !" No one made a bid. "Okay! Going . . . going. . . . Sold to the person with an ear for good music!" Greg yelled. Next to him, Karen scribbled the winning number down in a spiral notebook. "Now let's have an opening bid for a horseback-riding lesson with Diana Einerson!"

Again Torrey murmured to Katie. "And if you

fall off, Elise will come and sing to you in the hospital."

Katie's whole body vibrated as she tried to keep from laughing.

"Do I hear five?"

"Five!" a voice said.

"Six!" someone else called.

"Seven!"

Suddenly a thin, long-haired girl with braces jumped out of her seat. "Twelve!" she screamed.

A murmur went through the crowd.

"A horse fanatic," Katie said to Torrey.

He feigned a look of concern. "I hope she knows she's only bidding for a lesson, not the horse!"

"Now we're cooking!" Greg was saying. "Do I hear thirteen . . . ? No? Okay, sold for twelve! Hold up your number, please! All right, all you future English majors who're worried about graduating, here's your chance to bid on math tutoring from Frankie Baker!"

The football player in front of them whispered something to a friend.

"He wants to bid," Torrey said softly, "but first he has to find out what the word *tutoring* means!" They both cracked up. Despite a few slight twinges of guilt, Katie was having fun.

This time Zack McGraw called out, "Seven dollars!"

There were a few more bids, but Zack outbid them all and won it for ten-fifty.

The auction picked up speed. Greg read off the items with quick, corny jokes, and the spirit rubbed off on the crowd. Before long, just about everyone had jumped up to bid on something. Brian and Karen kept records of it all, and Holly and Colin helped by holding up silly visual aids, like a toy horse for Diana's donation and plus and minus signs made out of Styrofoam for Frankie's.

After about an hour, Katie's stomach started to hurt from laughing so much. Torrey had just threatened to bid for Karen's quarter-page ad so he could put in a picture of himself sticking out his tongue. She could just imagine what ultra-serious Greg would think of that. He'd freak!

"Now we've come to our last item," Greg announced. "And of course, it's mine!"

The audience cheered. "I'm so excited I think I'll faint," Torrey said.

"The winner will ride with me in my sailboat in the Potomac River Fun Race!" Greg continued. "So let's bid this one up! Do I hear five dollars?"

About a dozen programs flew into the air, almost all of them held by girls.

"Six dollars?"

Four more programs went up. People kept calling out bids up to twelve dollars. "Okay, I've got Eric Shriver with twelve buckos. Who's going to go higher?"

A voice shouted out, "Fifteen!"

Katie strained to see who it was.

"Let's see your number," Greg said.

Katie felt a knot in her stomach as Roxanne casually waved her program in the air.

"All right, going for fifteen dollars! Do I hear sixteen? Going . . . going. . . ."

"That smug little . . ." Katie whispered.

"Well, don't just sit there!" Torrey replied. He yanked Katie's hand in the air.

"I see sixteen in the back!" Greg said. "How about seventeen?"

"What are you doing?" Katie hissed to Torrey.

"Just livening things up a little." He waved his own program in the air.

"Seventeen in the back!" Greg announced. "Let's see your number!"

"Oops! I was just stretching!" Torrey called out.

"Seventeen!" Roxanne yelled.

Katie's anger began to well up inside. She gripped her program and stretched her arms up.

"I think I see a higher bid in the back again, but I'm not sure," Greg said. Katie lost her nerve and folded her arms. "No? Anyone for eighteen?"

As soon as Greg looked off to the left, Torrey popped up and down in his seat. Katie smiled, catching on.

"Looks like I have an eighteen! Hold up your number, please. . . . Didn't I see someone?" He shook his head.

"Eighteen!" Eric bellowed.

"Way to go!" Greg said, obviously thrilled. "Is that the high bid? How about nineteen?"

"Twenty!" Roxanne said.

"Great! Let's push it to twenty-one! Remember, it's all for the — "

Quickly, both Katie and Torrey bobbed up and down out of their seats, giggling.

"Hey, knock it off!" someone near them snapped.

There was a tense silence in the auditorium. Then, in a booming voice, Greg shouted, "Okay!

I've had enough! Will those people in the back stop messing around, or I'll have you both thrown out of here!"

Katie and Torrey both sank into their seats, red with laughter.

"I've got your twenty-one!" said Eric.

"Thank you," Greg answered, subdued. "All right, do we have the highest bid? Going, going. . . ."

"*Fifty dollars*!" Roxanne called out firmly.

Everyone in the auditorium began whispering. There was a smattering of applause and amazed whistles. Katie stopped laughing. All of a sudden it wasn't funny anymore.

"I think we have a final bid!" Greg shouted, as Karen slipped a piece of paper onto the lectern. "Going for fifty dollars! Going, going, gone! That's the end of the auction, and . . . uh, according to Karen's instant calculation here, we've gone *over* our goal by seventy-three dollars!"

A standing ovation swept through the crowd, and everyone joined — everyone except Katie, that is. She sat in her seat, steaming, while the auditorium emptied out.

"See what I have to put up with at home?" Torrey said. "My sister just won't lose. Come on, let's go."

"No! I want to wait," Katie said, on the verge of tears. "I don't want to see any of those creeps on the way out."

As the last people straggled out, Katie and Torrey walked into the hall. "Let's go out the back way," Katie said.

They took a left, and then another left down a

side hallway. Katie began to walk faster — she wanted to leave and fast.

But she and Torrey were only halfway down the hall when the side door of the auditorium flew open. A pair of laughing voices echoed through the hall.

Seconds later Katie came face to face with Greg and Roxanne.

The silence felt as if it would never break. Finally Roxanne said, "Look who my delinquent brother has hooked up with at the Hall of Shame." She stared at Katie through slitted eyes. "I can't say I'm surprised. He always attracts a certain type."

Katie felt as if she'd been slapped. She looked at Greg. In his eyes she saw a mixture of hurt, anger, and disgust. "Wh — what can I say, Katie?" he stammered.

Torrey spoke right up. "Hey, is our friendship any worse than yours, huh?"

Katie nodded. At least Torrey sticks up for me, she thought. "That's right!" she said. "But I guess you can't talk to me anymore now that I'm not the perfect, preppy, goody-two-shoes school leader that you are!" She laughed. "What are you complaining about, anyway? You've got the glamour-girl of Stevenson High drooling all over you! Come on, Torrey, let's go!"

"See ya later, Rox!" Torrey called over his shoulder as he and Katie continued down the hall and out the door.

Chapter
11

"And now we have a WKND exclusive — the final count of all the collected money from last week's Junior-Senior Prom Auction! As expected, just about every dollar pledged was accounted for — thanks to the deep pockets of some very generous students. . . ."

The sound of Josh's voice made Frankie cringe. In fact, she'd begun to dread lunchtime on days when Josh was on because she knew she'd have to listen to him. It was too bad, though, because his show used to seem like such a good excuse to tune out the bigmouths at the Stevenson upperclass table. Now Frankie just quietly ate her sandwich as the loud talk flew around her. She caught part of a conversation about a prom dress, listened vaguely to discussion on how to beat the system on SATs when you weren't sure of an answer, and another one about whether or not someone should apply to the University of Pennsylvania next year.

Frankie liked everyone all right, but every once in a while she wondered what it would be like to sit at another table. She gazed around to the other side of the cafeteria. There, Greg, Karen, Brian, and a few Stevenson kids were laughing and talking all at once. They looked like they were having so much fun. And more than that, Zack was sitting at the table. Jerko Zack, who was so perfect-looking but only wanted her for her brain! Frankie sighed. Some girls complain about being sex objects, she thought. Me? I'm a math object!

"Why the wandering eye, hmmm?" Roxanne nudged Frankie in the ribs. "Would you rather be sitting somewhere else? Discussing home runs with Zack the Jock?"

"Touchdowns," Frankie muttered.

"What?"

"I said touchdowns! Home runs are baseball, Roxanne! Touchdowns are football!"

"Ooh. Excu-u-use me! My, we *are* in a snit, aren't we?"

Right away Frankie felt guilty. "I'm sorry, Rox," she said. "I—I guess I'm just in a rotten mood today. . . ."

"Really? Why? You should be thrilled after that auction. Now you'll have more tutoring sessions with Zack!"

"Yeah, right."

Roxanne winked. "You want some advice?" Without waiting for an answer, she went on. "Take your glasses off and wear something a little more sexy. I could even lend you an outfit — my father sent me something that would be just right for you! Then, when Zack arrives, tell him your computer crashed, and go out to the movies!"

"Thanks, Roxanne, I–I'll think about it." She knew Roxanne meant well, but as usual, somehow her advice only made Frankie feel worse.

"Next up on the spring agenda is the Potomac River Fun Race, which is coming up this weekend!" Josh's voice continued to boom out. "Should be a strong showing by Kennedy this year. In fact, my unbiased prediction is that first place will go to the legendary *Sally Ride II*, manned, or should I say 'peopled,' by Greg Montgomery and Roxanne Easton!"

"Hey, hey! Someone's moving up in the world!" Daniel Tackett called to Roxanne, from the other end of the table. "Going out with one of the Kennedy honchos, huh?"

"Please, Daniel!" Roxanne said, with an impish smile. "We're just riding on the same boat. I happen to like sailing!"

Daniel put his hand over his mouth and guffawed, along with almost everyone else at the table.

"It's a really cute boat," Roxanne insisted, leaning over the table excitedly. "Greg says he's never lost a race with it!"

"Uh-huh, right, Roxanne," Daniel continued. "Only he's never had to sail it with someone clinging on to him the whole time!"

The whole table broke up laughing. Even Frankie joined in.

Roxanne laughed, too, until she noticed Frankie. Then she spun around and snapped, "Oh, I see your mood suddenly has changed. What a surprise! I didn't know you'd find *clinging* jokes so funny!"

Everyone stared at Frankie. She felt her face turning red. "Everyone *else* was — " she began to protest.

"Anyway," Roxanne went on, ignoring Frankie, "I expect *all* of you to be there to see us win! We need to see Stevenson represented — "

"Shh!" Daniel called out, waving his hand at Roxanne. "I want to hear this!"

The Stevenson table fell silent as they all listened to Josh on the radio:

"All in all, twenty-one responses were received! So it shouldn't surprise anyone that Karen's article is going on for wider fame! That's right, let's all wish her good luck in this most prestigious nationwide journalism contest — the Georgetown Journalism competition!"

"I don't believe this!" Daniel said, practically bursting with excitement.

"What's the big deal?" someone asked him.

"Wait! Wait! He's not done!" Daniel insisted.

"And I'd like to add a personal message of thanks and admiration to Lily Rorshack, for sharing the painful story of her life with us. We love you, Lil!"

Daniel hooted and clapped his hands. "HAH! This is perfect! 'The painful story of her life'! I love it!"

"Oh, no!" Roxanne moaned gleefully.

Frankie was horrified. She didn't see what was so funny. In fact, the whole thing seemed unbelievably cruel. She'd read that article and thought it was moving and sensitive.

About three or four others at the table obviously felt the same way. They just stared at Daniel in confusion.

"I think you'd better explain what happened," Roxanne said. "Not everyone knows."

"Okay, okay," Daniel said, practically gasping for breath. He motioned everyone to lean closer and listen. "You won't *believe* this."

Frankie pushed aside her tray and leaned over the table.

Daniel spoke in an exaggerated hush. "Well, when we all first transferred here, I was talking to Roxanne about the Kennedy crowd, and she told me all about how snobby they were. How they didn't want to accept us. Well, I didn't believe it until I went to talk to the editors of Kennedy's newspaper. You know, *The Red and the Gold*? Well, first of all, I've never seen anything so boring! So I told them exactly how they could improve it, and instead of listening to my ideas, they got all stuffy and weird on me. They thought they were way too important to listen to anything *I'd* suggest."

"*That's* no surprise," Roxanne agreed.

"What does all this have to do with Lily's interview?" Frankie asked.

"Well, I decided I'd have a little fun with them, give their paper a real shock. A hair-raising, breathtaking interview. The problem was, I needed a subject. So" — he looked around the table — "who better to call than the best actress in the history of Stevenson High — Lily Rorshack?"

A silence fell over the table.

"You're kidding!" someone finally said. "You mean that whole interview was. . . ."

"A fake? Of course! It was just a joke! Did you really *believe* Lily did all those things Karen wrote about in the article? I mean, come *on*! She's just the same as us — the most desperate thing she's ever done in her life is jaywalk!"

"But it sounded so real," Frankie argued.

"I know!" Daniel answered. "That's the best part. She treated it like an acting exercise — you know, creating a character, making up a history, getting into the emotions. She was sure Karen would catch on, but she bought it hook, line, and sinker. Lily was brilliant. She didn't even crack a smile through the whole interview. After it was over she felt so guilty, but I told her not to. I mean, any fool could tell it was a joke! It's Karen's problem that she believed it."

"I'm amazed you guys didn't know about it,"

111

Roxanne said. "We could have had you all complimenting Karen and writing those letters to the editor, like we did!"

"That was the best part," Daniel said. "Some of those letters were sappier than the article! I thought for sure they'd give it away! But *no-o-o-o*! Those pompous Kennedy creeps were walking around like they'd won the Pulitzer Prize or something! I thought nothing could top that, but now. . . . Who'd have thought that Karen's stupid little article would be entered in a *national contest*!"

A ripple of laughter made its way around the table, and everyone shot sneaky glances at Karen's crowd innocently talking across the room.

"Lily Rorshack's going to become an American heroine!" Roxanne said snidely.

"The cover of *Newsweek*!" Daniel added, doubled over with laughter. "I can just see it: 'The Amazing Saga of Shopping-Bag Lil!' "

Frankie looked around in disbelief. By now everyone was howling. Didn't anyone think the scheme was a little rotten? Were they all perverse enough to laugh at the fact that their little prank was going to get Karen in big trouble?

The scene made her sick to her stomach. She'd kept quiet for so long about all the backstabbing the Stevenson kids had been doing, but this was too much. She had to say something.

Frankie cleared her throat. "Um, I . . . uh, I don't know about this," she stammered. "I mean, someone's going to have to, you know, tell Karen the truth — "

"Oh, please, Frankie!" Roxanne cut in. "Don't be such a baby! Can't you see it's too late now? Let her believe it. It's not such a big deal!"

"Besides," Daniel added, "she deserves it. They all do."

Frankie knew he was wrong, but it was useless to argue about it. "Well, what about Lily then?" she asked. "Isn't somebody going to tell her? She still thinks it's a harmless joke. Don't you think she'd want to know that her 'life story' is going to be read by all these important people?"

Daniel frowned. "I didn't think of that," he said. "If Lily finds out how far this has gone, she'll freak out and tell the truth."

"She must be around here somewhere," someone at the table said. "Don't you think she heard the announcement?"

"No way," Roxanne answered. "She's been holed up in the auditorium every lunch period this week, working on her lines for *The Fantasticks*. She's playing the lead."

"That's right," Daniel said. "If we all keep our mouths shut, we can keep the whole thing from her until it's too late." He turned to Frankie. "That includes you. Don't worry, we'll tell Lily about the whole thing *after* the contest. By then she'll have no choice but to just forget it. Okay, Frankie? Promise not to tell?"

Frankie felt everyone staring at her. She knew what she wanted to say, but couldn't find the words.

"Frankie, I can't believe you're being like this," Roxanne said. "Daniel took you into his confidence, and now you want to betray him. How would you like it if I went around telling all *your* little secrets?"

"Wha—what secrets?" Frankie sputtered. Roxanne arched an eyebrow. Suddenly Frankie realized what she meant. Zack. "But . . . come on, Roxanne, I — "

"It's your choice, Frankie."

Before Frankie could respond, the bell rang. Roxanne scooped up her books and gave Frankie a meaningful look. With a clatter of trays, everyone got up from the table. Roxanne joined them as they charged away, laughing and joking.

Frankie just sat there and played with the crust of her sandwich, fighting the urge to cry.

Chapter
12

No matter how hard she tried, Frankie couldn't forget the lunchtime conversation. For the rest of the day, she did everything she could to take her mind off it — she raised her hand constantly in class, ran down the hall between classes, worked on homework in those few minutes before the teacher started speaking. She even threw herself into a softball game during gym period and almost broke her glasses in an outfield collision.

But now, walking down the hallway after Ms. Cathcart's class, her doubts came racing back. She could just picture Karen winning a prize in the competition, only to find out that she'd been lied to the whole time. How would she be able to keep her prize? How could she live with herself? And worst of all, what if one of the judges found out?

She walked straight to the computer room. It was her favorite place to think, to sort things out.

She flicked on one of the terminals and pressed a few buttons, calling up a "drawing" program so she could doodle on the computer.

I have to tell Karen, Frankie thought. I can't live with myself if I keep this stupid secret.

She used the mouse on her computer to draw an outline of a girl's face, with a glamorous, high-cheekboned profile and long, thick hair.

Then her confidence wavered. Daniel had told her in confidence, and besides, those guys would kill her if they found out she was the one who told Karen. . . .

She drew big, bushy eyebrows on the girl, and a black eye. Below the girl's nose, she drew a mustache and a beard.

But their whole attitude was so wrong. The Kennedy kids weren't snobby at all. Frankie remembered what a doll Jonathan was when they'd worked on those computer Valentine questionnaires together. And Katie was so friendly at the Fitness Center that time a while back — trying to talk her into going to the Valentine's Day Dance. Not to mention how sweet Diana was to her at the Maple Sugarin' Festival. . . .

The thing was, she wasn't really friends with Karen and her crowd. It was Roxanne and her friends who let her have lunch with them. What would she do, Frankie wondered, if they threw her out of their group?

With wild, jagged movements, she drew a thick cigar coming out of the girl's mouth, puffing clouds of smoke. She stopped for a moment and smiled at her creation. Then, with a glint in her eye, she wrote the name *Roxanne* below the drawing.

She couldn't help but let out a huge "Ha!" Immediately she covered her mouth and looked both ways, as if Roxanne would walk in any minute. She'd better get rid of it, she thought, poising her finger above the DELETE key. If Roxanne ever saw it, Frankie was doomed.

Suddenly Frankie pulled her hand away. No, she wasn't going to let Roxanne intimidate her. She and Daniel were wrong, and because of them, innocent people were going to be hurt. She had to go to the newspaper office and tell Karen.

She knew she might change her mind unless she acted fast, so she reached quickly over to the OFF switch. But she stopped herself just before she pressed it.

A small smile of triumph sneaked across her face as she looked at her unflattering portrait of Roxanne. With a firm thrust of her finger, she hit the SAVE button.

As Frankie approached the office of *The Red and the Gold*, she could hear the clacking of a typewriter. She paused at the door, psyching herself up, trying to ignore the inner voices that told her to run away.

With a burst of courage, she rushed into the office. "Karen, I have something to tell you!" she said.

"Oh!" Behind the typewriter, Emily jerked her head up and put her hand over her heart.

"Oops," Frankie said.

117

"You scared me!" Emily said. "I was all wrapped up in this article. Can I help you?"

"Sorry, I was looking for Karen. Is she around?"

"No, she left to visit Brian over at WKND. Do you know where that is?"

"Yes," Frankie said." Thanks."

Just when I get up enough nerve. . . . Frankie felt frustrated as she trekked down the hallway to the radio station. By the time she reached it, she was trembling. Nerves. She could just see the horrified look on Karen's face —

A low, smooth voice came out of the office, interrupting her thoughts. ". . . And so it was that Snub-Nose Pete, the cattle thief of the Midwest, was finally captured. . . ."

It's Josh, she thought. He was working on another story. Just what she needed: more cut-downs. Frankie could feel the anger rising to her face.

"No. No, that's not it," she heard Josh mumble. "And as the folks by the old fishing hole tell it, that's how Snub-Nose Pete met his match . . . in Raspberry Patch! Yeah! Much better!"

Now Frankie really felt like running away. All she needed was to be humiliated again. She stood still, not knowing what to do. If she left now, she knew she'd never get up the courage to tell Karen the truth.

She took a deep breath. *Okay, Frankie,* she said to herself. Don't let a little anger at Josh hold you back. Something more important is at stake here.

With that, she walked right into the office,

looked Josh in the eyes, and said, "Hi. I don't have much time. Where's Karen?"

Josh's face brightened up. He hopped out of his chair "Oh, hi, Frankie! Uh, I don't know where Karen went. She and Brian were just here a minute ago. I was trying out some material on them. . . ." He walked outside and looked up and down the hallway. "Hmmm. Well, I'm sure they'll be back any minute. They didn't say good-bye or anything. Come on in, rest your dogs."

"My what?"

He chuckled. "Dogs. That's Raspberry Patch lingo for feet."

Reluctantly Frankie walked into the office. How could he make fun of her one minute, and then be so nice to her the next? Maybe he *did* like her . . . a little. Josh plopped himself down on his seat by the booth and turned to face her. Frankie sat in the armchair farthest from him and waved for him to turn around. "You go ahead and keep working," she said. "I'll just — "

Frankie was cut off by a rustling noise, followed by giggling. She looked in the direction the sounds were coming from and saw the door to the record closet. It was closed.

There was an embarrassed silence in the office. Frankie and Josh both looked away from each other. Kissing noises and more giggling came from behind the door. She could feel her face heat up and begin to tingle. She knew she must have been beet red. Somehow, she was petrified to even look at Josh.

Just then the door burst open and Brian and

Karen emerged. Both of them wore strange, dreamy smiles. Brian's hair stuck out at funny angles, and Karen's beret was falling off. "We found that old Beatles album," Brian said, holding up a dog-eared copy of *Rubber Soul*.

"Great, Brian. That's just great," Josh said, trying to conceal a smirk.

"Hi, Frankie! I didn't know you were here," Karen said, looking from Josh to Frankie with a suspicious gleam in her eye. "Are you here to visit Josh? Brian and I can go over to the newspa — "

"No!" Frankie blurted out. "I'm here to talk to. . . ." Her voice trailed off. How could she spoil Karen's good mood?

Now Josh, Karen, and Brian were all giving her strange looks. It was either now or never. "I–I'm here to see you, Karen," Frankie said. "Th-there's something very . . . something very important I have to tell you."

Frankie was so nervous she could barely feel her fingertips. Karen must have noticed, because she knelt down on the floor next to her and gently touched her arm.

"What's up? Is something bothering you?" she said.

"Not me. . . . Well, yes, me! It's about your article . . . the interview with Lily. . . . She's not so different. . . ."

"What is it?" Karen said softly. "Do you know someone else like Lily?"

"Well, yes, that's it . . . sort of! I know a lot of people like Lily! I mean, not the way you think I know them. I mean, you know them, too, but you

120

don't know them the way you think you know them. I mean. . . ."

Karen smiled patiently. "Wait a minute, Frankie, slow down. What are you trying to tell me?"

Frankie felt as though she were a huge balloon attached to a running water faucet, and someone had just stuck her with a pin. The words came pouring out.

"I know you won't believe me, Karen, but you've got to withdraw the interview from the competition. It's a fake! The whole thing was an act. Lily wasn't abused as a child, she never begged on the streets, or lived in train stations. She made the whole thing up. But it wasn't her fault; I know it wasn't! It was Daniel Tackett's idea. He wanted to get back at *The Red and the Gold* staff because he thought you were all snobby. Or maybe he didn't really think so. Maybe he just believed rumors about you. I don't know! But either way, they were playing a joke on you. They even wrote those letters. I'm really sorry."

Frankie took a deep breath. On the one hand, a huge load had been lifted from her shoulders. She'd told them everything, and there was going to be no more agonizing. But on the other hand, she felt sick to her stomach. The look on Karen's face was like nothing she'd ever seen. All that patient understanding was gone. Now she looked stunned, almost as though she were in shock. Her eyes began to glaze over as she stared into the distance.

In a tiny, barely audible voice, Karen said, "Even the letters . . . ?"

"Are you sure about this, Frankie?" Brian asked. "This whole story could have been made up by someone who was jealous of Karen."

"I'm positive!" Frankie said. "I heard all about it during lunch period. When Josh made the announcement about the contest, Daniel thought it was hysterical! He bragged to everyone at the table about it!"

Karen silently stood up and began pacing back and forth. "The contest! I don't believe this. What am I going to do about the contest?"

"I'm sorry, Karen!" Frankie said, wishing she could take it all back. "I knew I shouldn't have told you — "

"No," Karen said. "I'm glad you did. Thank you, really. It's just that . . . well, I feel like such an *idiot*! I mean, I should have known. . . . I *knew* we should have done some more research . . . verified her — " Karen stopped abruptly. Her face was tight with panic. She pounded an armchair. "*Ooooohh*, that little sneak!" she fumed.

Brian reached out and tried to put his arm around her shoulders. "Easy, Karen, we can get it back — "

Karen shrugged off his arm and continued to pace. "Yeah? How? Sneak into the post office? It's too late, Brian. The deadline was today! The article is already there. This is it; I'm sunk!"

"Then I have another suggestion — just don't do anything," Brian said calmly. "I mean, you yourself said that your article probably won't win. So nobody will ever know, will they?"

Karen wheeled around at him. "Well, what if I *do* win, Brian? You know how many important people are going to read it, maybe even professors from *Brown*! They can take back my acceptance for this!"

"No way!" Brian said with a smile. "It's just not that serious! Let's just wait — "

"Not that serious?" Karen stared at Brian with wild eyes. "Not that serious? How can you be so cool about this, Brian? It's not serious to enter a totally false news article in an important contest?"

"Well. . . ."

"It's about as unethical as you can get!" Karen was screaming now. "People get thrown into jail for this sort of thing! Every ounce of me, every single inch of my entire being is completely offended!"

"Come on, Karen," Brian said. He reached out to her again. "Don't get so upset. . . ."

"Oh, I can't believe you said that!" Karen's eyes began to fill with tears. "Don't you touch me! I don't want your help, Brian! Not now, not ever!"

Choking with sobs, Karen ran out of the room and down the hallway.

Frankie looked at the floor as the room fell dead silent again.

Brian shrugged. "What can I do?" he said in a low, listless voice. "Well, I, uh, I'd better go." He stumbled out of the office, heading in the opposite direction from Karen.

This time Frankie was really alone with Josh — and she felt even less comfortable than before. She stared at her feet and tried to think of what to say.

Finally Josh broke the silence. "It's all my

fault," he said softly. "She didn't even want to enter the contest. I was the one who convinced her."

"Why did you do that?" Frankie asked.

"I . . . I really believed she'd win. It was such a strong feeling in my heart, you know? I guess I got carried away."

It was the first time Frankie had heard Josh sound so vulnerable, so gloomy. But he was right. If he hadn't encouraged her to submit the article, none of this would have happened.

"You and your dreams," she mumbled. "Your crazy, Raspberry Patch dreams."

She got up and walked toward the hallway. Just before she got to the door, she turned around one last time. She was really angry about the whole situation, and she had to let it out. "You think you can charm the whole world, don't you? You think life is like one of your neat little stories."

Josh's face drooped.

"Well, let me tell you something," Frankie continued. "Sometimes people like you only make things worse."

With that, she turned on her heel and left.

Chapter
13

Greg spun around as he heard the honking of a car horn. He waved and called out, "What took you so long? You missed the fun part — hooking up the trailer!"

"Sorry I'm late!" Roxanne replied, hopping out of her car.

Greg checked the trailer hitch one last time before giving his sailboat a pat. "There," he said. "We're mobile."

"Anything I can do to help?" Roxanne asked.

"Nope! We're ready to go!" Greg turned around. The first thing he noticed was that Roxanne was eyeing him from head to toe. He suddenly felt self-conscious, extra aware. But it was a good self-consciousness — Rox obviously enjoyed the view. As subtly as he could, Greg sucked his stomach in.

"I brought some goodies," Roxanne said, holding out a paper plate wrapped in foil.

What a hot-looking smile, Greg thought, watching her approach. She slinked toward him, her loose-fitting jumpsuit falling sexily off one shoulder. Coppery highlights shone in her hair as she tossed it lightly in the soft breeze. He took the plate when she held it out. "Great! What's in here?" he asked.

"Chocolate chip cookies," she answered. "I made them myself. It's fuel . . . for us."

"Thanks!" Greg said. "I think I'll save most of them for afterward, though. I don't want to weigh the boat down."

Roxanne laughed. "You're *so* competitive. Don't forget, Greg, this is supposed to be a *fun* race."

"I know. I can't help it. Just in my nature, I guess. I mean, sure it'll be fun, but won't it be even more fun to win?"

"I'm with you, Captain, and ready to go!" she said, giving him a little salute.

"You're going to go like that?" Greg said.

Roxanne looked disappointed. "Well, yeah! Is something wrong? Don't you like my outfit?"

"I love your outfit!" Greg said. "But . . . well . . . we *are* going to be on the water. Shouldn't you wear something a little less . . . uh . . . expensive?"

"We're not going to be *in* the water, silly," she answered. "A few little splashes won't hurt. Besides, I don't want to look like a slob when we go up to get our first-place trophy! I mean, *you* look good no matter what. . . ." She checked him out again with that same appraising smile. ". . . But sometimes *I* need a little help."

126

Greg chuckled. "Oh, no you don't!"

"Really?" Rox cooed, her face lighting up. She moved closer to him.

Greg began to feel a little flushed and uncomfortable, and he knew it wasn't just from the sun. He glanced at his watch. "Oh, wow! We only have a few minutes. Let's go!"

Hopping into the front seat of his mom's car, he started the engine. Roxanne went around to the other side. He honked the horn lightly, and his parents came out of the house. "See you at the race!" he called out with a cheerful wave and started off in the direction of the river.

"Let's get 'em!" Greg shouted as they pulled away. He let out a loud whoop.

"Yeah!" Roxanne echoed and clapped her hands excitedly. She looked over and gave Greg a winning smile. "*Nobody* can stop us now!"

Greg was starting to feel all pumped up about the race. Roxanne's obvious excitement helped, too. He was thinking about her differently today, now that Katie was out of his life. . . .

But as they got closer to the river, he couldn't help feeling a funny pang of sadness. A crazy wish that it was Katie who was going to be on that boat with him.

Roxanne's heart started to race as they came within sight of the river. A crowd of spectators had already formed on the grassy bank. "Oooh, Greg, this is exciting!" she squealed.

"Next stop, the Americas Cup!" Greg said.

Roxanne squeezed his hand, which made the color rise to his cheeks. She loved watching Greg blush. He was so smart and strong, but he also had a wholesome quality that reminded her of a Boy Scout.

As she got out of the car, a couple of cheers broke out from the crowd. She glanced over to see Daniel, Frankie, and a few other Stevenson kids on a blanket by the river. With a dramatic sweep of her hands, she blew them a kiss.

All around them sat the Kennedy crowd. Before long they started a rhythmic "Greg! Greg!" chant, clapping their hands in rhythm. Greg grinned and took a deep bow, then began to unhook the sailboat from the trailer.

"Everyone's here already!" Roxanne said as she watched Greg.

"Yeah, just about," he answered.

Roxanne thought she detected a little hesitation in his voice. She had already noticed that Katie was nowhere to be seen. He's still thinking about her, she thought. Quickly she changed the subject. "Did you check out Brian and Karen?"

"No, what about them?" Greg said.

"They're way over on the edge of the crowd, far away from everybody. They look like they're at a funeral or something."

Greg shrugged. "So what?" he said, emotionless. "They probably had a fight. It happens."

Roxanne *had* to get his mind off that girl. She leaned against the car and bit her lip. "I don't know, Greg. Everyone down there looks so . . . *experienced*. I just know I'm going to make a fool of myself."

Greg smiled as he got into the car to back the trailer down to the river. "No way, Rox. I mean, some of these people are really good, but a lot of them probably can't tell a schooner from a kayak. You'll look like a champ. All you have to do is move from one side of the boat to the other whenever I say."

"You're sure? I'm scared!"

"Positive!"

"Well, okay. . . . But after this is over, I may need to be taken on a picnic to eat those cookies."

Greg laughed. "It's a deal. Come on, let's go!"

He slowly eased his mom's Mercedes down the boat ramp. The sun reflected off the white letters that said *Sally Ride II* as the boat finally slipped into the river. Roxanne skipped down the ramp after him, carrying the sail bag. She watched Greg's biceps tighten and bulge as he set up the mast and boom. All around her, she could tell that other girls were staring at Greg and giving her the eye. Eat your hearts out, she thought.

"Okay, give me the sail," Greg said. After the sail slid up the mast, and Greg's car and trailer were parked, he turned to Roxanne and said, "You first, landlubber."

She nervously stepped inside. She looked up and down the bank. Dozens of entries were lined up, from rickety little canoes to big wooden rafts to sleek sailboats. There were even some bizarre creations like a queen-sized bed frame attached to pontoons and a huge, homemade paddleboat driven by someone with a handlebar mustache and a Gay Nineties bathing costume.

She watched Greg as he waited, one foot in the boat and the other on the grass, for the race to start. She could tell he was mapping out some sort of strategy, checking the wind and the current.

Soon a voice boomed over a megaphone: *"Ladies and gentlemen, prepare to launch."* Some last-minute stragglers rushed down to the edge of the water.

Greg shook his arms out as the yellow flag was raised on the committee boat.

"Sit back," he said.

The blue flag was raised. Five seconds. Greg leaned forward and tensed his leg. A bearded man on the committee boat slowly raised a starting pistol.

Bang! With a powerful push, Greg launched the boat into the river. He jumped inside and adjusted the sails.

"Can I do anything?" Roxanne shouted.

"Not yet!"

Greg caught the wind right away, and within seconds they were in the middle of the river.

"We're ahead! We're ahead!" Roxanne yelled.

"Duck!" Greg instructed her. "Lean to the right!"

She pulled her head down as the sail swung inches above it. The boat lurched to the left. "This is fun!" she exclaimed.

"You ain't seen nothing yet!"

On either side of them, boats came closer. Roxanne clutched the *Sally Ride II* as it sliced through the water. She watched Greg's face; he looked fierce and determined as he sized up the competition. For all Roxanne knew, this race *was* as important as the Americas Cup — at least to Greg. And they were going to win.

We're more alike than you think, Roxanne

wanted to say to Greg as she stared at his handsome face. We both go for the best!

"Yaaaaah! Where'd you get your license, at a K mart?"

"Ssshhh!" Katie said, dissolving into giggles. "You're terrible, Torrey! That poor lady didn't even see us!"

Torrey popped his head back in the window. "She still shouldn't have cut us off! Hey, look, we've got some open road!"

"So?"

"Come on, let's see how fast you can take this baby."

Katie laughed. "This isn't exactly a racetrack!"

Torrey slapped his forehead. "Ooooh! I almost forgot! I'm in the car with Little Miss Good Citizen!"

"Hey, wait a minute. . . ."

"What?" he said with a devilish grin. "Don't tell me you're actually going over thirty miles an hour!"

"We'll see about that," Katie answered, her eyes flashing. She gunned the accelerator and the car screeched down the road.

"WHOOAAA! GO FOR IT!" Torrey yelled.

Katie knew she could get into big trouble for this, but somehow she just didn't care. She'd always stayed out of trouble before and look where it had gotten her. Nowhere!

Flying down a flat stretch of road along the river, they sped past a small wooden building with a dock. "Wait! That's the place!" Torrey said.

Katie slammed on the brakes and yanked the

steering wheel to the left. The tires squealed. She felt the left side of the car practically lift off the ground as she made the sudden U-turn. With another burst of speed, she pulled up to the front of the little building and stopped short.

"You are *dangerous*!" Torrey said, grinning. He jumped out of the car.

"I was just getting started," Katie replied. But inside, all she could think was: I can't believe I did that! As she stepped out, her knees were even weaker than usual.

Torrey looked at his watch. "Hey, we'd better hurry. They should be coming by here any minute."

"Where's the finish line?" Katie asked.

"Way down there, where all those people are," he said, pointing about a quarter-mile down the river to where a large crowd was gathering.

"What are we going to do?"

"I don't know. Just razz my sister, I guess. If she hasn't fallen out yet, that is! Come on, let's hide behind the dock!"

They went around the building and stood by the dock, peering up the river for a glimpse of the *Sally Ride II*. Before long, a mass of boats appeared from around a bend.

"Look! They're way out in front!" Katie shouted. She knew Greg was doing all he could to win the race. She kept telling herself she didn't really care, but deep down inside there was a voice that wanted to cheer Greg on.

"Get down! Get down!" Torrey shouted. They hid behind the dock until they could see Greg's and Roxanne's faces through slats in the wood. Then they jumped out.

"Watch out for that log!" Torrey yelled.

The *Sally Ride II* pitched in the water as Roxanne swung around left and right. Seeing nothing, she looked over to the riverbank.

Torrey yelled, "What's the matter, Rox? Can't keep your balance?"

Roxanne put her hands on her hips and stuck her tongue out at Torrey.

"Looks like you're a real help!" Torrey jeered. "Tell your boyfriend if he dumped you, he'd win easily!"

Roxanne leaned out of the boat. Her face was scrunched up with anger. At the top of her lungs, she yelled, "Yeah? Well, I don't see you and that drippy little one-legged friend of yours out here!"

"*Duck, Roxanne!*" Greg cried as the sail came swinging around. Roxanne let out a scream and grabbed onto the boom. The boat teetered from side to side for a moment and stopped, as Roxanne finally got out of its way.

Torrey was doubled over with laughter, but all Katie could think about, over and over again, were the words: *drippy little one-legged friend*. She was so mad she could hardly see straight.

Out of the corner of her eye, Katie saw a little rowboat by the dock. An idea began to form. She nudged Torrey in the ribs. "Come on," she said, pointing to the boat. "Let's go out there."

Torrey did a double take. "Whaaat? Rent a rowboat? Now?"

"Not rent it, take it. Just for a minute. I *was* on

the crew team, after all. I should know how to row this thing out there. Besides, nobody's around — they're probably all at the finish line."

The corner of Torrey's mouth began to turn up in a smile. "Yeah," he said. "Let's do it!"

They ran to the boat — Katie limping the whole way — and jumped in. Katie grabbed the oars and rowed out into the river. "Tugboat coming to the rescue!" Torrey yelled.

Katie never thought she'd be able to catch Greg's swift sailboat, but they finally pulled up alongside the *Sally Ride II*. Greg was scrambling to adjust the sail. "What are you doing? You're crazy, both of you!" Roxanne screamed.

"Just thought I'd lend a helping hand!" Torrey said. He reached out and grabbed Roxanne's leg.

"No! No!" Roxanne tried to pry his hand loose. The two boats rocked back an forth. Katie panicked that the rowboat would turn over. She stood up and reached for the edge of Greg's boat.

"Cut it out!" Greg yelled.

Two other boats passed to their left, sending out ripples in the water. As the rowboat pitched up and down, Katie lost her balance.

"HELP!" she shrieked. Her foot slipped and she tumbled out of the boat and into the water, still clutching the side of the *Sally Ride II*.

"Whoooooaa!" Greg shouted as he lost his footing. Waving his arms helplessly, he went plunging into the cold river.

Somehow Torrey and Katie managed to get themselves back to the shore. Torrey planted his feet on the ground and shook the water from his hair like a dog. "We really drifted, didn't we?" he said. All around them, people were cheering their favorite boats as they crossed the finish line.

"I'm cold," Katie said. Her leg was absolutely killing her. It was a miracle she even made it to shore. Somehow the whole thing had stopped being fun. She was so angry at herself — angry mostly that she'd let her anger at Roxanne get out of control. "I'm going back to the car. If you want to stay here, you can get a ride with your sister."

"O-o-ooh, no!" Torrey answered. "I'm coming with you."

As soon as they turned to walk away, a booming voice rang out from behind them: "Katie! Wait a minute!"

Katie felt a chill run down her spine. Reluctantly, she stopped walking and looked at the ground. She heard footsteps pounding behind her, and before she knew it, she was face-to-face with Greg.

She looked up into his cold, accusing eyes. His teeth were chattering. She couldn't tell whether it was from anger or the cold river water. Clenching her teeth, she shrank away from him, knowing he would scream at her.

But with a hoarse, aching voice, he only said two words. Two words that sliced through her like a knife: "Why, Katie?"

All Katie could do was shrug her shoulders. How could she possibly explain everything that was racing through her head right now?

"Can't you say anything, Katie? Anything?" he said. Katie felt as if his eyes were burning right through her. "I can't believe the way you've changed! You've gotten so spiteful, so . . . so mean! Is this what happens to people who hang out at the Hall of Shame? They only want to tear things down, to make people's lives miserable?"

Katie wanted to sink right down into the ground and never come up. Instead she rocked lightly back and forth and said nothing.

"I lost the race, Katie. No, that's wrong — I didn't lose it, I gave up on it! It doesn't sound like me, does it? Is that what you want? You want me to turn into a loser, like you've become? Well, if that's the kind of life you want, you can have it! But I don't want any part of it — ever!"

Katie tried hard to fight back the tears as Greg stomped away. All of a sudden she felt as if her body had been taken over by an evil monster all these weeks, and now she'd finally gotten rid of it. It had drowned in the Potomac River. But Greg didn't know that. From now on, all he would see when he looked at her was that monster.

"Wow, was he mad!" Torrey said, laughing. "You should've told him it was Roxanne's fault. I mean, she was the one who rocked the boat."

Without a word, Katie started to walk away.

"Hey, what do you say we go for a ride downtown? They put in a great new video game at the Hall of Fame!"

Calmly, without the slightest emotion, Katie turned and said, "Let Roxanne take you. I don't feel like hanging out with you, not today or ever again."

Torrey began to sputter, "W–wait . . . you're

joking, right? Hey, you can't leave me here. Roxanne's gonna kill me! Not to mention that big dude. . . . Hey, wait! Wait!"

Katie never once looked back as she walked to her car and drove away.

Chapter
14

"Who would like to tell me the difference between a sine wave and a cosine wave?"

Frankie sighed and looked out the window. She hated review sessions, especially in math class. And especially with Ms. Cathcart's droning voice.

Tuning out the teacher's voice, she figured she might as well try to think out something that had been bothering her all weekend. It had hit her when she saw the expression on Karen's face at the boat race. She looked so dull, so blank, as if there was just no use being alive.

Frankie could understand *why* Karen was upset, but there was something more to it. Something was *wrong* about Karen's reaction. Frankie just couldn't put her finger on what it was.

"Hmm? Don't all put your hands up at once," Ms. Cathcart droned on. "Has everyone given up?"

All of a sudden the answer hit Frankie over the head. That was it, she thought. Karen had just *given up* on her problem. So had Brian.

A picture of Roxanne and Daniel and the whole Stevenson lunch table popped into her head. Just like I've given up on myself, she thought sadly.

The whole thing was so confusing. It didn't seem right to just throw in the towel about a problem, but what if the problem was so big you just *had* to give up? That was a depressing thought. Slowly, her mind started to wander, to think of a different world, one where Frankie was stunning and Roxanne didn't exist. She thought of a soda shop in a beautiful little town, and a noon whistle. . . .

Suddenly Frankie snapped out of it. She shuddered. That was *certainly* not the answer, she thought. Not Josh Ferguson's silly dream.

But what was the answer? To just sit around while the Daniels and Torreys and Roxannes of the world stomped all over everybody? Frankie began to steam up inside. An image kept coming back to her, something she'd seen at the race. It was an image of Torrey and Roxanne sitting on their boats in the Potomac and trading stupid insults while poor Greg and Katie floundered in the water.

Enough was enough. She had to do something — too many people were being hurt. She didn't know Katie or Greg enough to help them out, but at least she could try to convince Brian and Karen to do something about that article.

When the bell rang, she ran right over to the

newspaper office. Maybe she'd be lucky and find both of them there.

She rapped on the door and Dee Patterson opened it. "Hi, Frankie, what's up?" she asked.

"Is either Karen or Brian here?" Frankie asked.

Dee rolled her eyes. "I wish. I haven't seen Karen since the middle of last week. I don't know if she's too busy studying or what, but if you find her, tell her to get down here! We need her desperately!"

"Okay. Thanks, Dee." Frankie rushed over to the WKND office to look for Brian. There she saw Josh sorting out a stack of records with Alex Aldrich.

"Hi, Josh," Frankie said. She couldn't help noticing how cute he looked.

"Hey, Frankie. Just a second. . . ." He turned to Alex and said, "Look, I give up. I can't figure out this crazy system of Brian's. Could you go to the front office and ask them to lend you a stack of blank labels? I'm just going to mark these myself."

"Sure," Alex said, and he hurried out the door.

"Sorry, Frankie," Josh said. "But things are crazy around here. Brian hasn't been showing up to do *Soundings* since that whole thing about Karen's interview. Guess who's had to do the news *and* music during lunch?"

"I *thought* I noticed something different about the show," Frankie said.

Josh beamed a wide, little-boy grin. "You like my taste in music, huh?"

Frankie didn't particularly want to get into a

conversation. "Well, actually, I was wondering why the songs were so old-fashioned."

"Oh, come on! You don't like the theme from *Love Story*? It's a classic!"

Frankie smiled. She was still a little mad at Josh, but there was something about that face, something so sweet and trusting. . . .

"I guess it's silly to ask if you've seen Brian or Karen, isn't it?" Frankie asked.

Josh burst out in hysterical laughter. "Oh! That's the *silliest* thing I've ever heard! Have I seen Brian or Karen? What a joke!" Then he abruptly folded his hands and quietly said, "No," with a sincere, innocent expression.

Frankie couldn't help laughing. "Be serious, this is important!"

"What's so important? They cancel the Georgetown contest?"

"No, but . . . but. . . ."

Josh looked at her expectantly.

"We have to help Karen, Josh! If I can't find Brian, it's going to have to be you and me!"

Josh looked surprised. He gave her a sad smile and shrugged his shoulders. "You're looking at the wrong guy, Frankie. I'm the one who started this whole mess. I'm keeping my nose out."

Frankie threw up her hands. "You're just like the rest of them," she blurted out. "Go ahead, just sit around like a lump when something bad happens. Don't even *try* to make things work!"

"Well, what could I do to help, Frankie? I have no idea!"

Frankie slapped her math book down on the

table. "Let's think of something." She paced back and forth.

"We could call a private detective. . . ."

"Why?"

"I don't know . . . that's what they do in the movies."

"Great, Josh. Next thing I know you'll suggest that we break into the contest headquarters — " Suddenly Frankie stopped in her tracks. "That's it!"

"What?"

"If Karen's article isn't there, no one will ever read it, right?"

"You mean sneak into Georgetown University and steal the article? You and me? You're joking!" He turned and smiled at Frankie. Instantly the smile turned to a look of disbelief. "You're not joking."

"It's the only way, Josh! It's perfect! We'll pretend we're thinking of applying there next year. Once we're there we can figure out a way to get into the contest office. There must be a stack of submitted articles there — and we'll just *un*submit Karen's!"

Josh shook his head. "Look, Frankie. You were right when you said I was a dreamer, that all I know how to do is make up stories. But my stories are *make-believe*, Frankie! I could *never* do anything like this!"

"Why not?" Frankie demanded.

"Sorry, it's just too insane — even for me."

Just then Alex came back into the office with a small yellow box. "I got some labels," he said. "Where should I put them?"

"Here, let me show you," Josh said. He turned away from Frankie and went over to the pile of records.

Frankie felt shocked — shocked that she'd stood up to Josh like that, and shocked that she had thought of such a crazy idea. But at the same time, she knew she was right. For the first time in her life, she didn't feel one shred of self-doubt. She really wasn't being crazy at all. In fact, it seemed like she was the only sane person in a world gone topsy-turvy.

Frankie thought of Roxanne and Daniel, imagining how they would react if she went through with her plan. Some of the old feelings rushed in, and for a moment she was overcome by horrible fears. But she blocked them out. She knew that if she turned back now, she'd be a doormat for the rest of her life. A scared little puppet living in Roxanne Easton's shadow.

"Josh," she called out, "I need to speak with you."

"Hang on a minute, Alex," Josh said. He followed Frankie into the hallway. "What's up? Did you think of something a little more reasonable?" he said.

"No," Frankie said firmly. "I just wanted to let you know that I'm going, Josh, whether you come or not. Wish me luck."

She didn't even give him a chance to answer as she turned and walked away. In her heart, Frankie knew that without a second person to help out, her idea was ten times as farfetched. But by the time she was halfway down the hall, she could barely feel her feet touching the ground. Even if

143

it didn't work, she thought, it would be the most useful thing she'd ever done in her life.

Suddenly she heard the thump, thump, thump of sneakered feet behind her. "Hey, Frankie!"

She turned to see Josh running toward her.

I will not allow him to talk me out of this, she vowed to herself. "What do you want?" she called out.

Huffing and puffing, he adjusted his glasses and pushed his mop of curly hair away from his face. "Wait up, will you? You can't do this all alone!"

"I've made up my mind, Josh."

"Don't be ridiculous!" he said with a big smile. "I'm coming with you!"

Chapter
15

Josh shivered as he drove up the hill to the Georgetown campus. "Can you shut your window a little?" he said.

"It's seventy-three degrees out," Frankie said absentmindedly as she looked out onto the street.

"Oh. It just . . . seems cooler, I guess." Josh was nervous. He imagined the two of them as undercover agents, disguised as high school kids by an expert plastic surgeon, driving incognito into a secret enemy stronghold. But the scenario was too close to the truth for him to enjoy it.

"There's a spot!" Frankie shouted.

Josh jammed on the brakes. Both he and Frankie lurched forward.

"What are you doing?" Frankie said.

"Sorry. You scared me."

"Come on, Josh, get it together. We can't let anyone suspect what we're up to."

"Right, right," Josh answered. He drove up to

the empty space. After about three tries, he managed to parallel park.

As they got out of the car, Frankie opened up a fold-out map. "We're right across from this gate," she said, pointing to a spot.

Josh looked around for evil, suspicious faces. Surely a journalism professor was spying on them.

"Pay attention, Josh," Frankie demanded.

"Oh, sorry." Josh spun back around, trying to look as nonchalant as possible. He didn't want to blow their cover by seeming too anxious.

He watched as Frankie pointed at another place on the map. "Now, the mailing address of the contest was the journalism department, which is right *here*. It's just across the circle." She gave Josh an intense, excited look. "Ready?"

"Ready, chief," Josh replied. He pulled up the collar of his jeans jacket and took out a pair of sunglasses from his pocket.

Frankie laughed. "Knock it off. The look doesn't go with tie-dyed high tops."

Josh looked self-consciously at his sneakers. She was right, he thought. He should have on a pair of fashionable Italian loafers. Spy shoes.

He followed Frankie across the street and onto the campus. The bustle of the street faded away, replaced by peaceful chirping of birds, and the shouts of students throwing Frisbees across the lawn. The maple trees had light, spring-green leaves, and Josh had the urge to wander around. Maybe he should apply here, he thought, looking at the stately gray stone buildings.

"Come *on*, Josh! Don't float away!" Frankie called, already halfway across the circle.

Josh ran after her, and together they walked into the journalism building. The lobby was full of students rushing back and forth, clutching books and notebooks. "What room number?" Josh whispered.

"Just follow me," Frankie said. She climbed a flight of stairs to the second floor. Josh tiptoed behind her, making sure to check around in case someone was sneaking photos of them. You never knew.

Frankie led him to a closed door at the end of the hall. "Now," she said. "Just keep your eyes open and go along with everything I say. And *don't* space out. We'll play it by ear."

Josh nodded. He held his breath and tried to look as innocent as possible. Frankie pulled back her hair, cleared her throat, and knocked firmly.

"Come in!" a female voice called out.

Frankie pushed open the door. They walked into a medium-sized outer office with beige walls and a well-worn gray carpet. On their left, a white-haired secretary smiled up at them from a pile of papers on her desk. Behind her, way off in the far left corner of the office, another elderly woman clacked away at a computer. An open doorway on the opposite wall led into an empty larger office with wood paneling.

Beware of the innocent old ladies, Josh thought to himself. They're always the toughest.

"Can I help you?" the closer woman said. Josh smiled and let his eye wander around the room while Frankie did the talking.

"Yes . . . uh, my name is Hildy Muldoon and

147

this is my brother. I'm, um, thinking of applying to Georgetown. . . ."

An exasperated sigh came from the corner, and Josh looked back to see the other secretary furiously pressing on the same key, over and over.

"I . . . I'm interested in majoring in journalism," Frankie continued, "so I thought I'd — "

"Ooooh! There it goes again," the other lady muttered, loud enough to interrupt Frankie. "What did I do *this* time?"

The white-haired woman held up a finger and said sweetly, "Would you mind taking a seat for a minute, dear? I think we're having a slight problem." She got up and walked back to the other secretary. "What happened, Harriet?"

Josh and Frankie sat down in a couple of vinyl chairs against the wall. "Now what?" Josh said.

"Just hold on," Frankie answered.

They watched as the white-haired woman stood over Harriet's shoulder and stared at the computer.

"It just won't *do* anything, Vera," Harriet complained. "Every time I try to call up the professor's appointment calendar, the whole darn thing just freezes!"

"Did you try pressing the Escape button?" Vera asked. "That worked the last time. . . ."

Suddenly Josh noticed Frankie's eyes brighten. She leaned closer to him and said under her breath, "The important stuff must be in the other office. Wait for the right moment, then go!"

"The right moment?" Josh whispered frantically. "Wait! What am I supposed to do?"

But it was too late. Frankie was walking back

to the two old ladies. Great instructions, he thought. What was she going to do — slip a sleeping pill into their peppermint tea?

"Excuse me," Frankie said cheerfully, "can I help?" The two ladies looked up, their brows knitted with frustration. It dawned on Josh what she was up to. Brilliant decoy, he thought. So professional, so smooth.

"Oh! Are you one of those young computer whizzes?" the one named Vera asked.

Frankie smiled. "Well, I do know something about computers. What's the problem?"

Josh sat tight. This was going to be tricky. Both women were sitting sideways to him. Even though they were way in the opposite corner, they'd see him in a second if he tried to sneak into the inner office.

"These darn things are supposed to *save* time, but you spend so much time trying to figure them out," Harriet complained. "It's this appointment calendar, you see. . . ."

While Harriet explained, Josh stood up and sauntered around the room, trying to seem as though he were wandering aimlessly.

"No problem," he heard Frankie say. "Let me set up a program for you. You see, first of all, you want to put the appointment calendar in the computer's resident memory. . . ."

Josh glanced over at Frankie. She was standing directly on the side of the two ladies, boxing them into the corner. Neither of them could possibly see him enter the office now. He felt his palms begin to sweat. Okay, Josh, he said to himself, it's hero time. Silently he ducked into the inner office.

Once inside, his heart pounded like mad. He inched along the wall and froze, half-expecting someone to pop out of the shadows. With a gulp, he gazed around the dark, oak-paneled room. He crouched down and spread his arms out, low to the ground, just as he'd seen James Bond do in the movies. The room seemed clean — no sinister men in wide-brimmed hats, no slinky female counterspies, no trapdoors, or hidden cameras. Just a desk, bookcases, and a windowsill piled high with papers.

He cautiously approached the windowsill. There were at least a dozen stacks of paper, each one about two feet high. He flipped through a couple of them. With mounting dread, he realized they were *all* newspaper articles — news, features, sports, and interviews. Could they be the contest submissions? he wondered. It would take him half an hour or more to sort through them!

He realized this was going to be impossible. Frankie could never stall those ladies long enough. Josh started to walk back to the outer office. The sound of Frankie's voice carried clearly into the room, with a background of fast computer keys. Josh stopped just before the door. If he came out empty-handed, she'd never speak to him again. With a sinking, trapped feeling, he turned back around. He'd do it, but never, never would he allow himself to be talked into this again.

Suddenly something on a bookcase caught his eye — four neat wire baskets, each marked with identical yellow index cards. He squinted and read one of the cards: GJC ENTRIES.

The letters sounded familiar: GJC. He repeated

them in his mind, trying to figure out what they stood for. His eyes widened as the answer hit him. Of course! Georgetown Journalism Competition!

He ran over to the stacks and riffled through them. They couldn't have been better arranged. The biggest one contained news articles from local high schools. One was about a Vietnam memorial, another about a lawsuit, but no interviews. The next pile was just sports.

Josh felt his blood race as he looked at the third pile. Feature articles. He tore through them as fast as he could. There was an interview with a local TV star, a play review, a humorous essay about an indoor mall. . . .

All of a sudden Josh felt like screaming with joy. There it was, right in front of his eyes, inches from his fingers! "Close-up: Lily Rorshack" by Karen Davis.

He was about to pull it out when he heard a voice. It was an old, tired voice, and it sounded like it was coming closer. "Let me just make sure I didn't erase any of the professor's personal appointments. I'll get his calendar from the other office."

"Wait!" Frankie's voice rang out. Josh's heart stopped. He was dead now. There was no way out. He wondered what kind of food they served in prison. Frantically, almost without thinking, he dove under the desk.

He heard the padding of footsteps suddenly stop. "That's funny. I thought I saw something move in here," he heard Vera say. He peered out from under the desk to see a pair of sensible black shoes quickly joined by Frankie's sneakers.

"Well, uh, staring at a VDT for a long time can do that to you," came Frankie's voice. "Anyway, you don't need that calendar. Come back and let me show you how you can recover anything you've ever lost. This is *really* useful."

Josh watched as both pairs of feet disappeared. Then, as quick as he'd ever moved in his life, he ran to the stack again, pulled out Karen's article, and stuffed it down the back of his shirt.

He dashed over to the door and pressed himself against the wall beside it. Frankie was explaining something hopelessly complicated. Slowly, he inched his face around the doorway and looked inside. Frankie was gesturing over the keyboard and telling both of the ladies to try out a set of commands. Again, her body blocked their view of him.

As silent as a cat, Josh sneaked out of the inner office and kept going, right out into the hallway. He crumpled onto the floor, exhausted, just as a man in a lightweight wool suit appeared around a corner. Approaching Josh, he chuckled and said, "You look like you just ran the marathon."

Josh smiled and watched as the man walked through the door. With a jaunty "Hello, ladies," the man strolled into the inner office and sat down at the desk. Josh felt a shudder run through him as he leaned back against the wall. If he had stayed in the office only a moment longer. . . .

Before long a smile crept across his face. I did it, he said to himself. Just like in the movies. I carried out a dangerous act of unselfish heroism!

A deep chuckle welled up from inside him. He

closed his eyes. He could hear the title of his next radio show: "The Raspberry Patch Newspaper Caper."

Frankie thought she would never stop laughing. Hand in hand, she and Josh raced across the lawn.

"WEEE DID IT! WAHOOOO!" Frankie hollered.

"YEEEE-HAA!" Josh bellowed. "Good work, *Hildy Muldoon*!" He jumped high into the air and tried as hard as he could to click his heels.

Frankie pulled Josh across the lawn, practically making him fall on his face. Josh caught up and grabbed her other arm. Together they swung each other around in a circle, bursting with joy. At first Frankie was aware of the curious stares from the people around her, then she saw only a blur as they went faster . . . faster. . . .

Before she knew it, they were on the ground, dissolving into dizzy, giddy laughter. But when Frankie looked over at Josh, she realized she was staring into the handsomest face she had ever seen.

Frankie rolled closer to him, her mind reeling and her heart pounding from so much laughter. Josh rolled, too, and suddenly they were eye-to-eye. The silence was electric. Before Frankie could think about what was happening, she and Josh were wrapped in each other's arms. His passionate smile was the last thing she saw before her eyes closed in a tender, heart-stopping kiss.

She felt as if the two of them were suspended in outer space, like a planet all their own, just floating forever. She didn't want their lips ever to part. She wanted to stay like this forever, re-membering how every inch of her body felt, memorizing every tingle that shot through her.

When they finally, gently pulled apart, they still clung to each other. Frankie sighed and buried her face in his chest. The whole world could have been watching them and she wouldn't have cared.

"That was wonderful," Josh said softly.

"Mmmmm," was all that Frankie could manage to answer.

"The whole day was wonderful, Frankie. I . . . I know I've been a dreamer all my life, but it was because real life just seemed so boring in com-parison. Until today." He squeezed her even tighter. "I never actually thought I could *live* a dream. I never thought I'd do something heroic, or have something like . . . like this, like you. It's all because of you, Frankie."

He pulled away from her and looked into her eyes. "Even if you don't believe me, Frankie, even if you think my stories are the dumbest things in the world, I *know* that you're twice as beautiful as that girl at the soda fountain. Twice as brave, too. I'll always believe that."

Frankie wanted to cry. For the first time, she began to believe him, too.

After a long, dreamy rest, they walked back to the car. But Frankie noticed a change in Josh. A sudden quietness had come over him.

She looked up at him and ran her fingers through his hair. She was so content being with Josh that she couldn't believe she hadn't fallen instantly in love with him. But no, she'd hung around mooning over Zack, who thought of her as a great math tutor, and a good advice giver. But Frankie was over Zack now — finally. She'd found a great guy. And Josh wasn't just cute and good-looking. He liked her, too. "I have an ending for your story," she said with a smile.

"What story?"

"You know, the one you told last week? The one you asked people to submit an ending for?"

"Oh, right. Nobody sent in a good response."

"Well, how's this?" She imitated Josh's radio voice, "The next time the heartsick, shy boy went into Pop's Soda Fountain, the sweet girl threw her arms around him and said, 'You did it, shy boy, you gave me spring fever!' "

Josh looked as if he wanted to say something, but he just grinned.

"What? Don't you like it?" Frankie said.

"It's great," he answered distractedly.

Frankie couldn't figure out Josh's mood. "Is something wrong?" she said.

By now they had reached the car. Josh silently unlocked her door, then went around to the driver's side. Frankie kept staring at him, wondering what was on his mind.

After they both got in the car, Josh finally turned to her. "Promise me you won't laugh."

"I promise," Frankie said, giggling.

"You laughed!"

"Sorry!" Frankie puckered her lips, trying to keep a serious look.

"Well, I was thinking, um, I hadn't really planned, you know, too many weekends in June, and, like, some are still free, and I noticed one of them is — " He suddenly stopped short. Frankie had never seen him so tongue-tied. "I know you probably wouldn't dream of saying yes, but will you go to the prom with me?"

Frankie looked into his vulnerable brown eyes. "I wouldn't dream of saying anything else *but* yes, Josh. Yes! Yes!"

And just as she thought nothing could ever equal that kiss on the lawn, Josh drew her face toward his and proved her wrong.

Chapter
16

Frankie couldn't wait for lunch the next day. By the time the bell rang to end her fourth period class, she practically rocketed into the hallway.

Josh was already in the WKND office when she got there. He was sitting in front of the booth, gesturing to Alex, who was inside. "Put your mouth closer to the mike . . . that's it!" he said into a headphone mike. "Don't worry, just read the notes, *slowly*. You'll be great." He caught a glimpse of Frankie and waved. "This will only take a second," he whispered to her.

Frankie looked at her watch. She figured that Karen would be getting to the cafeteria just about now.

"Okay, ten seconds . . ." Josh said to Alex. "Nine . . . eight. . . ."

Frankie shifted from one foot to the other impatiently. She was glad Josh had gotten out of doing his show today, but she wished he didn't have to train someone who'd never broadcasted before.

"On the air!" Josh said. The sound-effects intro to the news came through the loudspeakers — a corny electronic-music piece set to the rhythm of typewriters.

"Go!" Josh said.

The next thing Frankie heard was a sound like an airplane crash. Alex was clearing his throat right into his mike. Then a squeaky, nervous voice came through the speakers.

"Uh, welcome to Alex Aldrich, with *Jokes and Cloaks*. In today's news. . . ."

Josh gave the thumbs-up sign and darted out into the hallway with Frankie. "Well, it's a start," he said. "I think he'll be fine until Brian gets here."

"Do you have the article?" Frankie asked eagerly.

Josh stopped short and slapped his forehead. "Oh, *no!*" Frankie felt her spirits suddenly sink. Then Josh turned to her with a devilish grin and said, "Of course I do!" He pulled a sealed manila envelope out of his pocket. On it he'd written:

KAREN DAVIS
C/O WKND
KENNEDY HIGH SCHOOL
ROSE HILL, MARYLAND

Giggling, they ran to the cafeteria. The Kennedy crowd was already starting to gather at their table in the center of the room, but Karen wasn't with them. Frankie ducked around to check the hot lunch line, but Karen wasn't there, either. She surveyed the room one more time. The Stevenson bunch was off in their usual corner, with Roxanne and Daniel leading the conversation. Frankie was about to look away from them when she noticed one solitary, sad-looking person sitting at an empty table next to the Stevenson table.

"There she is!" Frankie whispered to Josh. "In the corner."

Josh chuckled when he saw her. "I hope we don't spoil her bad mood."

They hurried across the cafeteria. Josh sat down next to Karen, and Frankie took a seat across the table.

"Hey, Karen, how's it going?" Josh asked.

"Fine," Karen mumbled, barely looking up.

Josh and Frankie exchanged a sly glance. "Josh found something in the radio station mail addressed to you today," Frankie said matter-of-factly.

Josh thrust the envelope toward Karen. She lifted her head and looked at it with a blank, slightly sour expression. "Why would anyone send something to me at the radio station?" she asked.

"I don't know," Josh said. "Why don't you open it."

"Wait a minute, there's no postmark." Karen said. "And the return address is Raspberry Patch! Is this one of your crazy jokes, Josh?"

Frankie bit her lip as Josh shrugged. Karen tore open the envelope and pulled out the article. Her

159

jaw fell open in shock. In a hushed voice, she read the Post-it note Josh had attached: "Compliments of Hildy Muldoon."

Slowly the look of shock changed as her mouth curved upward, almost as if her muscles had forgotten how to smile. Tears started to roll down her cheek as she leaped up from the table and threw her arms around Josh. "My article!" she cried. "This is it! This is the copy I sent to Georgetown!"

"Yes, ma'am!" Josh said as Karen squeezed him and rocked back and forth. "Mmm, I ought to do this sort of thing more often! This is fun!"

"Hey! Watch it!" Frankie said jokingly, her hands on her hips.

Karen let go of Josh and wiped the tears away. "Oh, Frankie," she said, "you must have had something to do with this!" She ran around the table and gave Frankie a hug. "But *how* in the world did you do it?" She looked at the article. "And *who* is Hildy Muldoon?"

Frankie laughed and said, "I'll tell you over lunch, but you won't believe me." She looked lovingly at Josh. "Anyway, you'll probably hear a better version of it tomorrow on *Cloaks and Jokes*. With the names changed, of course!"

"Ooh, go get your lunches, quick! I want every detail!" Karen said. She flashed a deliriously happy smile at both Josh and Frankie. "You two are the best! I don't know how I'll ever pay you back!"

Suddenly Josh heard the intro music to *Soundings* over the loudspeaker. "Oops, time to go," he said. "Got to give my assistant a pep talk about his debut!"

160

Frankie looked over at the lunch line, which had dwindled down to almost no one. "I'll be right back," she said. She hurried toward the counter, right past the Stevenson table, which was dead silent.

"*Pssst*," a voice to her left hissed. Frankie looked over to see Roxanne, signaling her over to an empty spot against the far wall.

This is it, kiddo, Frankie said to herself. You knew this was coming sooner or later. She trailed Roxanne obediently, rehearsing what she would say.

When they got there, Roxanne turned around and smiled. A little too casually, Frankie thought. She seemed a little too tense.

"We missed you at lunch today," she said.

"Oh, sorry," Frankie answered. "I had some stuff to do."

"Mmmhmm." Roxanne answered with a nod. She looked at her fingernails. "I, uh, saw you and Josh talking to Karen."

"That was us, all right."

"So . . . what was this 'stuff' you had to do?"

"Nothing much. . . ."

"Nothing much? That's nice to know. You didn't tell her our little secret, did you?"

Frankie was silent.

"You didn't! Frankie, answer me!"

Frankie shrugged her shoulders. Then she nodded, weakly. She couldn't lie to Roxanne.

Roxanne looked as if she'd just been punched in the stomach. Her eyes were wide with shock. In a muted, hurt voice, she said, "Ooh, you little sneak! How dare you turn on us like that, your *best* friends?"

"Roxanne, I — I — " Frankie stammered.

"I guess you're too *good* for us now, aren't you! You want to worm your way into that little Kennedy clique, don't you! Well, let me tell you something. I know them real well now, and they'll never accept someone like you. Where will you be when they reject you? Huh? Answer me that, Frankie!"

Frankie just shook her head. A few days ago, she would have been mortified if Roxanne had yelled at her like this, but today she couldn't have cared less. Instead of backing away, Frankie stood right up to her old friend. She looked her straight in the eye, matching her strong, hateful stare. And in that glance, she saw something she'd never seen before. Roxanne was scared of her.

That was all Frankie needed. In a firm, clear voice, she said, "You can yell all you like, Roxanne. It's not going to change anything. Karen knows about the whole thing. Not only that, she's got the article back. Josh and I went to Georgetown and got it out of the competition! And you know what? I don't care *what* you think of me — or what any of your petty little friends think. I'm tired of your lying, and I'm tired of you trying to make *me* feel bad because of your ego."

Roxanne began to sputter. "Wha — How — You can't speak to me like that — "

Frankie cut her off. "Sorry, Rox. I can speak any way I want. If you don't like it, you know what you can do about it!"

Roxanne's face turned white as Frankie

marched off across the cafeteria. The farther away Frankie got, the happier she became. She felt herself bouncing up and down with joy, and she even didn't care if that made her look like a boy. Roxanne had told her that, so it didn't matter. In fact, it didn't matter what *anyone* thought. People were going to have to take her the way she was. If they didn't want to, it was their tough luck.

Frankie was feeling about twenty feet tall, when she was suddenly stopped by a strong, muscular hand. She looked up to see Zack smiling at her.

"I've got to speak to you," he said.

All of a sudden, everything she had just been thinking went flying out the window. Her heart began to race. His eyes were so full of confusion, and so . . . *blue*.

"Can we meet after school?" he asked with a warm, vulnerable smile.

"Af–after school?" Frankie stuttered. "Today?"

"Yeah, over by the quad. Same place as last time." He gave her a wink.

Frankie gulped. Talking to Zack made her head spin. For a long time she didn't say a word. Finally, she got control of herself. In a soft voice she said, "Zack, if you need a tutoring session, see me after social studies class tomorrow for an appointment." Then she stared him firmly in the eye. "But if you're just looking for a shoulder to cry on, I think you'd better find yourself another girl. I'm sorry, Zack."

His dumbfounded expression didn't bother Frankie a bit as she headed right to the end of the lunch line.

Chapter
17

"Yeah, that's my favorite song. Wish I could play it again, but believe it or not, it's that time already. So till tomorrow, this is Brian Pierson with *Soundings,* signing off for myself and WKND's newest newscaster, Alex Aldrich!"

Brian. Just the sound of his name gave Karen a little jolt. She had almost completely forgotten about him, about how miserable their relationship had become. For the last half hour, she had been deliriously happy. It was as if she'd been living under a storm cloud for a whole week, only to have the sun suddenly burst through. Throughout Frankie's story she had been totally absorbed, asking her again and again for details. The whole thing was so crazy, so hard to believe; she had to look at her article every few seconds just to convince herself she wasn't in some bizarre daydream.

But as she walked out of the cafeteria and began to think about Brian again, her mood sank. Their last date, the boat race, was about as romantic as a funeral. She wondered if he really cared about her anymore. He'd seemed so cool about her problem, telling her she was being too emotional, not really bothering to understand what was going on inside her. Maybe it was just as well all of this had happened, maybe it was a sign that she and Brian weren't right for each other.

Karen knew that it was time to clear the air. If they were going to break up, she was determined it wouldn't be through cold silence. She headed straight for WKND office. It was a trip she used to make every day after lunch, but for the last few days she hadn't gone. She'd been too depressed and angry. Besides, deep down inside she wanted to see if Brian would come to her. In all this time, he hadn't.

She knocked on the radio station door. Should I tell him about Josh and Frankie right away? she asked herself. Quickly she decided no, that would make it too easy for him. He'd think everything was fine again. She wanted to make him squirm a little, to tell her exactly how he felt. After all, if he could love her in the good times, he should be able to love her in the bad times, too.

The door flew open. It was Alex, beaming from ear to ear. "Oh, hi, Karen!" he said exuberantly. "That was me on *Cloaks and Jokes* today. Did you hear it?"

"Uh, yeah, I sure did. Great job." Karen tried

to look over his shoulder. "Is Brian around?"

"No. He ran out of here right after the show. Maybe he had a test or something."

"Oh . . . uh, fine," Karen said, turning to leave.

"Is there something you want me to tell him?" Alex volunteered.

Karen shook her head. "No, just tell him I'm looking for him."

"All right, I will," he said.

Just then a voice boomed out from behind Karen: "There you are!" She spun around to see Brian trotting toward her.

"Hey, Brian, Karen's looking for you!" Alex shouted. With a mischievous grin, he shut the door, leaving the two of them alone in the hallway.

"I was just looking for you, too," Brian said.

"I guess that means we have a lot to talk about," she said dryly.

"Yeah, I . . . I guess we do."

"You first."

Brian ran his hand over his hair. He looked from side to side, then at his feet. He cleared his throat. When he spoke, it was in a tense, low voice. "Uh, I've been thinking a lot about what's happened the last few days, ever since you found out about the interview being a fake. I . . . I guess it's made me think a lot about us. Things just aren't . . . you know, the way they used to be. What I mean is, I think we both know this isn't working out. . . ."

"Yes," Karen whispered. Her glasses slipped down her nose as she looked at the floor. She hadn't expected it to happen this way — that

Brian would be the one to break up with *her*. Somehow it didn't seem fair. She braced herself for the bad news.

"So . . . I guess what I'm trying to say is I hope you'll forgive me. I was really being a jerk, Karen, and I'm not sure why. I shouldn't have been so laid back when I knew you were upset. I think I just felt so, you know, powerless or something. I'm not used to feeling that way."

Karen looked up. She couldn't believe what she was hearing.

"I know how horrible you feel," he continued, "and I want you to know I feel horrible about it, too. The whole thing *is* really important. And scary. I'd be petrified if I were in your shoes. So, well, if you still want me to, I want to help you get back your article."

All of a sudden, Karen felt like throwing her arms around him. He was trying so hard and he really *did* care! She tried to look him in the eye, but he was too nervous to return her glance. She smiled to herself and decided to have a little fun.

"Well, I don't know, Brian, would you be willing to go to Georgetown to get the article back?"

Brian nodded. "Yes," he said softly.

"If you had to, would you find a way to sneak into the journalism office and look for it?"

"If I had to, I would!" He gave her an earnest, loving look.

"Good, that's just what I want you to do," Karen said. She reached into her shoulder bag. "Now don't forget, it looks just like this." She pulled out the article and handed it to him.

He leafed through it, a puzzled expression on his face. "What did you do, type it over again? This looks like the real thing!"

Karen smiled happily as Brian stared at her, wide-eyed. He looks so cute like this, Karen thought. But she couldn't string him along any further. "It is the real thing. Josh and Frankie already went and got it for me!"

"And you were just . . . ?" Brian cocked his head and gave her a half-embarrassed, half-accusing smile. "You little. . . ."

Karen screamed as he wrapped her in a bear hug and swung her around. "Why didn't you tell me?" he said. "You just wanted me to sweat, didn't you? You just wanted to have fun!"

Karen snuggled her face into his broad chest. "Oh, come on, Brian, do you have to take it so *seriously*?" Suddenly she broke away and dashed down the hall, giggling.

"Oooooh, I'll get you for that!" he shouted, taking off after her.

Their laughter echoed through the hall as the bell for the next class rang.

After school that day, Karen walked to the office of *The Red and the Gold*. She was dying to tell everyone what had happened. It felt as if she hadn't seen all her old friends in months. For the first time since the whole problem with the article happened, she was excited about writing again. Her head was bursting with new ideas, and she was sure one of them would be the best article she'd ever written in her life. Unfortunately, the truly best one was the one she knew she could never write: a true-to-life account of Frankie and Josh's heroic deed at Georgetown! She laughed to herself at the thought of writing it and submitting it to next year's Georgetown competition.

As she approached the office, she noticed it sounded awfully quiet. Usually the editors were clacking away at their typewriters by now. She grabbed the doorknob and burst into the office. "Anybody home?" she called out cheerfully.

Four solemn-looking heads turned to look at her at the same time. All of the editors were sitting on folding chairs, gathered in a circle. There was a strange tension in the air, and no one greeted Karen. They all just glanced at each other uncomfortably.

"Oh!" Karen said. "Am I missing an editorial meeting? I–I didn't know. . . ."

The agonizing silence continued a few seconds until Dee said, "Uh . . . you didn't know, Karen, because this meeting is about you."

"Me? What do you mean?" Karen felt a lump form in her throat. Something very strange was going on.

Pam, Emily, and Adam Tanner shifted uncomfortably and looked at Dee. "Well, it's just that, like, we were trying to decide about the rest of the year's issues. And, you know, we realized it's the end of the year, and people have priorities and all, but it's been really tough this week. And, well. . . ." She fidgeted and looked around.

Finally Emily said, "What Dee's trying to say, Karen, is that it doesn't seem like you really want to be a part of *The Red and the Gold* anymore." Karen started to protest but Emily cut her off.

"It's okay, really! Believe me, we all understand. I mean, you've gotten into Brown, you've already written the best article of the year. . . . We were just meeting to figure out how to, you know, divide your work between the rest of us."

Karen didn't know how to react. She'd been so wrapped up in her problems, she hadn't stopped to think how many people had been affected by her bad mood. It all made perfect sense. They had an issue to put out, and Karen had been off in another world the whole time! She hadn't wanted to even *think* of the newspaper, especially since it was a newspaper article that got her into the whole mess in the first place!

She looked around. Everyone's eyes were glued to her. It looked like a meeting of the Joint Chiefs of Staff, trying to decide a matter of grave national importance. Suddenly, the whole situation struck Karen as being very funny. Slowly, without meaning to, she began to chuckle. As she looked from one concerned face to the next, it grew into a full-fledged laugh. The editors stared at her with bewildered expressions. Some of them laughed self-consciously. Others just gaped.

"Oh, I'm so, so sorry!" Karen blurted out. "I've put you all in such a bad position. Please forgive me!"

"What's been *with* you, Karen?" Dee demanded.

Patiently, Karen told them the whole story. They all were dumbfounded as she told of the deception by Daniel and the rescue mission by Frankie and Josh. By the end of it, most of them were hopping mad.

"This is outrageous!" Emily said. "You poor thing, having to be dragged through all that. No wonder you were so depressed!"

"I tell you," Pam added. "That Frankie Baker is really terrific! I always thought she was a good kid, but I never knew she had such guts! I could *never* have done that."

"Well, I think it's disgusting she had to do it at all!" Emily cut in. "How dare Daniel pull a stunt like that! Are those the kind of articles he used to print in the Stevenson newspaper?"

Dee nodded. "One thing I know for sure, he just blew his chance to ever write for this paper! You know, we tried so hard to include him and his friends in all our activities, and look what happened. As far as I'm concerned, we should all be on our guards around them from now on."

Everyone agreed, including Karen. At that moment, she wasn't feeling too charitable toward the Stevenson gang. If this is the kind of relationship they all want with Kennedy, she thought with a sigh, then this is what we'll give them.

Chapter
18

"How's this, Katie?" Her blonde pigtails shaking from the effort, a thin underclassman tried valiantly to lift herself into an arabesque on the balance bean.

"Arch your back and keep your head up!" Katie called out. The girl has talent, she thought, but no technique. She was aching to go up and demonstrate, but as always, a vision of Dr. Merwin's stern face glowered at her like an angry ghost.

Sometimes Katie wondered why she even bothered coming to practice. It was impossible to concentrate and even more impossible to watch girls with perfectly healthy bodies being so sloppy and awkward. But what else could she do? She didn't want to sit around at home, she wouldn't dream of going to the Hall of Fame again, and Greg hadn't even looked at her since the weekend.

Even though four days had passed since the

race, the thought of Greg made Katie squirm with embarrassment. She had asked herself at least twenty thousand times why she did what she did. She kept playing the race over and over in her mind, as if it were one of those video games with multiple-choice endings. In one ending she knocked Roxanne off the *Sally Ride II* and rode with Greg to the finish line. In another she threw Torrey into the river before they even thought of taking the rowboat. But when the mental tape ran out, she was always left with the truth. She had really blown it. Greg would never speak to her again, and even if he did, she wouldn't be able to look him in the eye.

And that wasn't all, Katie realized. *Everybody* saw what happened, and of course they must have swarmed around Greg after the race. By now all of them had probably heard his side of the story and seen his hurt, angry face. All week long, she'd felt the accusing stares of people in the hallway. She'd practically memorized every tile on the floors from looking down so much.

" 'Atta girl, Stacy! You're starting to look like Katie out there!" she heard Coach Muldoon call out. For a moment, Katie's gloom lifted. She smiled at the compliment.

"Hey, hey! That was great!" Katie shouted. She walked over to Coach Muldoon.

"Wouldn't hurt if you gave her some encouragement," the coach said under her breath. "She really idolizes you."

Katie laughed. "Come on, Coach. You're just saying that to make me feel better!"

"Hey, take the compliment while you can,"

Coach Muldoon replied with a wink. "I can butter you up when I don't have to coach you!"

Katie felt warm inside as the coach went back to her job. No wonder she hung out here, she thought. It was the only place where she still had a decent reputation.

She climbed up on the bleachers and suddenly became aware of a pair of eyes following her, peering in from behind the gym's glass doors. Her heart sank when she realized it was Molly. Oh, please leave me alone, Katie thought. The last thing she needed was to be yelled at by her former best friend.

Katie pretended not to notice Molly. She leaned forward as if she were concentrating hard on the girls. Every few seconds she shouted words of encouragement or advice. But Molly just came into the gym anyway. She waited beside the bleachers.

"Good girl, Melissa — perfect arms! . . . Don't lock those knees, Amy! . . ." It was no use. Molly knew that she must have seen her by now. Quickly, as if she only had a second, Katie gave her friend a distracted little wave. She hoped that would make her go away, but it only seemed to bring Molly to life. She skipped up the bleachers and sat down next to Katie.

"Mind if I join you?" Molly asked.

"I guess not," Katie answered. She kept staring out at the gymnasts, but at this point she couldn't concentrate on anything. She just wished Molly would get whatever she wanted off her chest, and then leave.

"You haven't been very easy to track down, you know," Molly said. "Do you realize we haven't talked since that day out in the quad? What was that, like two, two and a half weeks ago?"

Katie was on the verge of exploding. "Okay, Molly," she said, trying to keep calm. "I know it was you who tried to bring me and Greg back together that day. And I know Greg told you what happened, finding out about the Hall of Fame and me running away and all. And in case you're going to ask, Yes, it was me who tried to mess up the auction, and yes, it was me who toppled over Greg's boat in the race, okay? And I know that makes you feel stupid for trying to patch things up in the first place." She looked Molly straight in the eye for the first time. "And all I can say is . . . I'm sorry. I don't know what's h–happening to m–me." Her lips started to quiver. "C–can we go over to the side of the bleachers so everyone won't see me like this?"

Molly grabbed Katie's hand and led her into a secluded corner behind the stands. "It's all right, Katie, I'm not here to yell at you. I want to help."

Molly's face seemed to shine like the sun. Her broad smile and open arms were the most welcome things Katie had seen in weeks. A tear rolled down her cheek as she let her head fall on Molly's shoulder.

"Oh, Katie," Molly said gently, "I can see how torn up you are inside! Won't you tell me what's going on? All week long I've wanted to talk to you. You need help. I have eyes, K.C. I know you haven't been yourself lately. . . ."

Katie sniffled and looked into her friend's deep blue eyes. As always, they seemed so full of understanding. "You can say that again. I . . . I don't understand it myself, Molly. I've been doing so many stupid things. It's like, it's like there's something big and ugly inside of me that wants to destroy everything I love. I'm afraid to talk to anyone now, to even look at anyone. . . . I mean, first I tried to blame it on my broken leg, then I blamed Roxanne for stealing Greg away. But it's *me*, Molly," she said through her tears. "It's *me* who's causing all of this!"

"Shh, shh," Molly said in a soothing voice. "It's okay. Katie, you've got to forgive yourself! I mean, let's face it, you're human, right? We all can go a little crazy when things get rough. When my father died, I ran away from home. I wrote my mother a nasty note saying I hated her guts and never wanted to see her again. You think that wasn't crazy?"

"I know. But everything worked out for you," Katie said.

"Yeah, it did. Luckily I realized my mother and my friends still loved me, even after all that."

"You really were lucky. I don't even want my friends to see me. I'm so embarrassed."

Molly handed Katie a kleenex. "Everyone still asks about you. They still care about you."

"Yeah, right. They ask if I've done any more stupid stuff."

"That's not true! They all ask me where you are, how you're doing. Really! They know some-thing's wrong, Katie. They're not stupid." She looked Katie straight in the eye. "Believe it or not, they want you to feel better."

Hearing that, Katie couldn't hold herself back

any longer. Her chest heaved as she sobbed into Molly's shoulder.

"Go ahead, let it all out. I need a new blouse anyway," Molly said.

Katie began to giggle. Or maybe she was still crying, she couldn't tell. All she knew was that she hadn't felt this happy since before her accident.

"About Greg," Katie said after a minute. "Is he . . . is he all right?"

Molly shrugged. "He'll live. But I have to admit, I can tell he's hurting. After all that work he did to pull the auction together and raise all that money, he told me he isn't even going to the prom."

"Not even with. . . ."

"Roxanne?" Molly said with a wry smile. "Be real, Katie. She was never Greg's type."

Katie gave her friend a sad look. "Could you do me a favor? I mean, I know Greg won't even look at me anymore, but will you . . . will you tell him I'm sorry for everything I did?"

"Well . . . it is against my principles. But I guess I will," Molly answered. "You are my pal, after all."

"Thanks, Molly. You know, you are the truest friend I could ever imagine!"

Molly smiled. "Well, you have no idea what an improvement it is to see you looking happier." She reached for her shoulder bag. "Listen, I have to go now. Will you be — " Suddenly her eyes widened. "Oh! I almost forgot! I brought you something."

She pulled a wrinkled piece of paper out of her

bag and gave it to Katie. "I found it in the student council room one day. I think you'll recognize the style."

Katie unfolded the paper. It was a smudged pencil drawing, a silly cartoon of a girl swinging over a giant gymnastics horse that was really a building. She wiped her watery eyes and looked closer. A pleasant shiver ran through her as she realized the building was Kennedy High, and the girl was *her*! "Greg drew this," she whispered.

"I guess he was saving it for some romantic moment," Molly said.

"I guess," Katie answered, her voice tinged with sadness. "Too bad that moment never came."

"Oh, you never know what'll happen," Molly said, walking toward the door. "You could always sell it if Greg becomes famous!" With a smile, she disappeared into the hallway.

Katie folded up the drawing and stuck it in her shirt pocket. Good old Molly. She can laugh her way out of anything. What a great outlook on life. Katie wiped her eyes and walked back around the bleachers into the gym. The last couple of girls were picking up their shoes and heading back toward their lockers.

When the girls were gone, Katie sighed and looked around the empty gym. She loved the peaceful, exhausted silence, that familiar pungent smell of a hard workout, the equipment stained with chalk dust.

Silently, cautiously, she went over to the balance beam. She ran her finger along the top and looked both ways across the gym. Carefully, she bent her knees and bounced lightly. It didn't hurt.

A smile flickered across her face. She pulled off her shoes and socks. Her heart began to pound with a secret, hidden joy. As she hiked herself onto the beam, she could hear the muffled sound of voices, the announcer calling out "*Kay-tieeeee CRAW-ford!*" and the swell of cheering from the crowd.

For the first time in months, she brought herself to a familiar standing position high above the rubber mat. And although she could only inch her way across, one foot slowly in front of the other, her arms straight out to the side, she felt stronger than she'd ever felt in her life.

Chapter
19

Walking to school that Friday, Frankie couldn't stop grinning. She knew she must have looked like a total goon, but she didn't care. For the first time she could remember, she was actually excited about the weekend. Not just looking forward to it — she often looked forward to spending Saturdays or Sundays working on crazy new software programs. But this was different. This time she was actually tingling all over just from the thought that she'd be walking into the sub shop after school with Josh. And that was just the start; on Saturday they were going to the Cherry Blossom Festival in Washington. They hadn't talked about Sunday yet, but Frankie had hopes for that, too.

As she got closer to school, she began to sing. Imagine, me singing aloud in the street, in public, she thought. The worst voice in the history of

Rose Hill. I could get arrested! She laughed. It was either that or scream out loud, and let the whole school know the big secret she was keeping from them. Something that only she could see. When other girls saw Josh, they didn't seem to look twice. The same way boys acted with Frankie. But what none of them saw was that Josh was the most attractive guy in the school. Nobody could match his brain and his sense of humor. Nobody had that cute mop of hair, that little-boy smile, those goofy worn-out sneakers he clomped around in. Only Frankie had bothered to look close enough to see all these things — all the wonderful things she once hated about him.

This whole week she couldn't get enough of Josh. Listening to *Cloaks and Jokes* became one of her favorite parts of the day. But actually being together was so much better. They always made sure to see each other every morning before school in the quad. The only problem was that she had to share him with the Kennedy crowd. She didn't mind that too much, though; it made her feel so warm inside that the crowd had accepted her so completely. They all had such a great time. Josh would always make everybody laugh so much they practically had to crawl to homeroom.

Frankie skipped around the side of the school. She could tell she was early; not too many students were hanging around the school. As the quad came into view, she saw only a couple of kids gathered in the Kennedy crowd's favorite spot. She was ready to run right over, when she heard a voice behind her.

"Hey, Frankie!"

She turned around. It was Roxanne, leaning against the side of the building. Frankie didn't know what to do. They hadn't talked since their argument in the cafeteria, and the last thing she wanted to do now was continue it.

"Come on over!" Roxanne called out.

Frankie had half a mind to just ignore her, but with a deep sigh, she realized she couldn't. Even though she couldn't stand Roxanne right now, it didn't give her a license to be mean to her. Dragging her feet, Frankie slowly walked up to her former friend.

Roxanne's eyes were distant and icy. "It's been a long time," she said.

"Yep."

"Are you still talking to me?"

Frankie thought that was a strange question, considering that Roxanne had been ignoring her all week. "I thought you weren't talking to *me*."

Roxanne nodded, as if she were deep in thought. "Yeah, I guess I was being a little moody this week . . . but I think you know why, Frankie. I was angry at you. I've been thinking a lot about it, though . . . and . . . well . . . I've decided our friendship is still important. . . ." She looked down at the ground and shifted her books from arm to arm.

Incredible, Frankie thought. An apology from Roxanne? All of a sudden she felt a wave of sympathy. Maybe they could patch things up and stay friends after all.

Roxanne straightened up and looked Frankie in the eye. "So I've decided to give you a second chance. I know you're probably been feeling miserable all week after all the rotten things you said. I mean, who wouldn't? But I guess today's a lucky day for you — I'll accept your apology."

Frankie felt as if she'd been slapped. It was a feeling that had become all too familiar around Roxanne. "What apology?" she said. "I haven't apologized."

Roxanne's eyes burned with anger. "No kidding, Baker. Take the hint. I'm letting you say you're sorry, okay? Do I have to spell it out for you?"

Frankie shook her head and met Roxanne's stare. "No, Roxanne, I understood you the first time. In fact, I understand more about you than you think. You think you can control me, don't you? Just like you think you control all those guys. Well, guess what? They may let you, but I won't. Not anymore. You want to be my friend, Roxanne? Well, then you can treat me like a friend, with caring and respect for who *I* am. If you just want someone to jump every time you say jump, go buy yourself a golden retriever!" Adjusting her shoulder bag, Frankie turned toward the quad.

"Wha — Don't you dare just walk away from me!" Roxanne shouted, her face fiery-red. "You realize I may *never* forgive you now!"

"Fine." Frankie shrugged her shoulders. "To be honest with you, Roxanne, I really don't care."

"Oh, yeah?" Roxanne called back to her, with a smug grin. "Well, don't come crawling back to me when you feel lonely, when no one will talk to you except those pimple-faced computer nerds!

Think about it, Frankie, what real friends do you have besides me?"

Frankie looked over into the quad. There, by the blossoming cherry tree, were Brian, Karen, Dee, Marc, and Elise, waving to her. Beside them, Josh was busy acting out a story. Frankie felt full of pride as she waved back. With a funny double take, Josh spotted her and winked, grinning from ear to ear.

She laughed. "Believe it or not, Roxanne, I have plenty of friends now. They're nicer to me than you ever were. And in case you didn't notice, I have a wonderful new boyfriend . . . *and* a date to the prom." Frankie stood up tall and smiled, letting the full weight of the words sink in. "Tell me, Rox — what exactly do *you* have?"

Roxanne was speechless. Her eyes were burning with rage and frustration.

Calmly, Frankie began to walk away. And she never looked back as she strode happily into the quad.

Coming soon ...
Couples #31
Prom Date

Lily craned her slender neck, scanning the cafeteria for signs of the ominous, monstrous "crowd." She didn't see any group that looked half as dangerous as the one Roxanne had described. "Who exactly is 'the crowd'?" she asked, still looking for Karen, whom she remembered from the interview, and Frankie, who was apparently the crowd's newest inductee.

"You know: Greg, Jeremy, Holly . . ." Roxanne rattled off the names, counting them on her fingers.

Lily wrinkled her nose. "Not their names, their faces."

She'd spent most of her time since the transfer at the Little Theater, and while she'd made some new friends in the drama crowd she hadn't been playing much attention to the Kennedy social scene at large. She couldn't have picked out Greg or Jeremy or Holly from among the cafeteria's occupants if her life depended on it.

Roxanne pointed with one coral-colored finger-nail. "There," she said.

Lily looked where Roxanne was pointing. At a large round table in the corner she saw Frankie and her new boyfriend, and Karen and *her* boyfriend from the radio station. And more people that she didn't recognize, and . . . Lily's heart leaped and then fell. Sitting between two strangers was the boy she'd been looking for all week, ever since she'd met him in the costume room at the theater. *Jonathan.*

"That boy . . ." Lily began, "Jonathan, I think? The one with the brown hair and the blue oxford shirt. Is he part of the crowd?"

Roxanne's next words were crushing. "*Part* of the crowd? He *is* the crowd!" She scowled.

"Oh," Lily said out loud. Inside she thought dismally, *Oh, Jonathan.* Her heartbeat had slowed, and now she could have sworn she could feel it break just a little. She'd found Jonathan, only to discover that he belonged to the crowd that hated everyone from Stevenson. The boy whose gray eyes had sent stars flying into her own had turned out to be Public Enemy Number One!

True love!   **Crushes!**   **Breakups!**   **Makeups!**

Read about the excitement—and heartache—of being part of a *couple!*

Order these titles today!

☐ 33390-9 #1 **CHANGE OF HEARTS** Linda A. Cooney
☐ 33391-7 #2 **FIRE AND ICE** Linda A. Cooney
☐ 33392-5 #3 **ALONE TOGETHER** Linda A. Cooney
☐ 33393-3 #4 **MADE FOR EACH OTHER** M.E. Cooper
☐ 33394-1 #5 **MOVING TOO FAST** M.E. Cooper
☐ 33395-X #6 **CRAZY LOVE** M.E. Cooper
☐ 40238-2 #15 **COMING ON STRONG** M.E. Cooper
☐ 40239-0 #16 **SWEETHEARTS** M.E. Cooper
☐ 40240-4 #17 **DANCE WITH ME** M.E. Cooper
☐ 40422-9 #18 **KISS AND RUN** M.E. Cooper
☐ 40424-5 #19 **SHOW SOME EMOTION** M.E. Cooper
☐ 40425-3 #20 **NO CONTEST** M.E. Cooper
☐ 40426-1 #21 **TEACHER'S PET** M.E. Cooper
☐ 40427-X #22 **SLOW DANCING** M.E. Cooper
☐ 40792-9 #23 **BYE BYE LOVE** M.E. Cooper
☐ 40794-5 #24 **SOMETHING NEW** M.E. Cooper
☐ 40795-3 #25 **LOVE EXCHANGE** M.E. Cooper
☐ 40796-1 #26 **HEAD OVER HEELS** M.E. Cooper
☐ 40797-X #27 **SWEET AND SOUR** M.E. Cooper
☐ 41262-0 #28 **LOVESTRUCK** M.E. Cooper

Complete series available wherever you buy books. $2.50 each

**Scholastic Inc., P.O. Box 7502, 2932 East McCarty Street
Jefferson City, MO 65102**

Please send me the books I have checked above. I am enclosing $_____
(please add $1.00 to cover shipping and handling). Send check or money order—
no cash or C.O.D.'s please.

Name_____

Address_____

City_____State/Zip_____

Please allow four to six weeks for delivery. Offer good in U.S.A. only. Sorry, mail order not available to residents of
Canada. Prices subject to change.   **COU987**

CHEERLEADERS®

Don't miss any exciting adventures of the popular Cheerleaders of Tarenton High!